Crazy Runner - Trailblazer - 1750

ൟ

RALPH E. BOWMAN

PublishAmerica
Baltimore

© 2010 by Ralph E. Bowman.
All rights reserved. No part of this book may be reproduced, stored in a retrieval system or transmitted in any form or by any means without the prior written permission of the publishers, except by a reviewer who may quote brief passages in a review to be printed in a newspaper, magazine or journal.

First printing

This is a work of fiction. Names, characters, places, and incidents either are the product of the author's imagination or are used fictitiously. Any resemblance to actual persons, living or dead, events, or locales is entirely coincidental.

PublishAmerica has allowed this work to remain exactly as the author intended, verbatim, without editorial input.

Hardcover 978-1-4560-1910-5
Softcover 978-1-4560-1911-2
PUBLISHED BY PUBLISHAMERICA, LLLP
www.publishamerica.com
Baltimore

Printed in the United States of America

Table of Contents

Chapter 1—Timothy 7
Chapter 2—Running Away 10
Chapter 3—Kituhwa 13
Chapter 4—The Tests 17
Chapter 5—Rifle 21
Chapter 6—Exploring 24
Chapter 7—A Bear 27
Chapter 8—White Men 31
Chapter 9—Change 35
Chapter 10—Shawnee 37
Chapter 11—The Village 41
Chapter 12—Creek 45
Chapter 13—Rapids 49
Chapter 14—Big Jim 55
Chapter 15—Traveling 59
Chapter 16—Land 63
Chapter 17—Finding a Trail 68
Chapter 18—Headwaters of the Ohio 71
Chapter 19—The Trip Begins 75
Chapter 20—Heading North 81
Chapter 21—Snow 85
Chapter 22—Massacre 90
Chapter 23—A Bigger Massacre 93
Chapter 24—Saving a White Man 102
Chapter 25—Survivors 106
Chapter 26—Dangerous Journey 109
Chapter 27—Warning the Settlers 115
Chapter 28—Christmas 119
Chapter 29—Kithuhwa 122

Chapter 30—Chickasaw 125
Chapter 31—A-wi U-s-di 130
Chapter 32—The Ceremony 134
Chapter 33—Challenge 136
Chapter 34—Traveling Again 140
Chapter 35—Slave 142
Chapter 36—Heading North 145
Chapter 37—Wolves 148
Chapter 38—Ohio 152
Chapter 39—Finding the Plantation 156
Chapter 40—Supplies 160
Chapter 41—Wounded 164
Chapter 42—Safety 169
Chapter 43—Thieves 172
Chapter 44—Careless 177
Chapter 45—Young Hunter 181
Chapter 46—Rescue 185
Chapter 47—Traveling 188
Chapter 48—More Settlers 194
Chapter 49—A New Home 202
Chapter 50—A Decision 207

Chapter 1—Timothy

Timothy was a good-looking boy. By the time he was 13, he was already taller than most men. He had long light brown hair and was very slender. He never wore shoes, which had made his feet very hard. He lived on the Violet Plantation, which was about 50 miles northwest of Charlestown in the Carolinas. The plantation was named after Mr. Cook's mother and the violet flowers growing all over the plantation.

He was intelligent and had eyesight that was above average for finding game. His superior eyesight was the reason that Mr. Thomas Cook, owner of the Violet Plantation, always took him with him when he went hunting. Mr. Cook had taught him to shoot a rifle, which was something at which he excelled. Several times, he had asked Mr. Cook where he had come from and Mr. Cook always had the same answer, "Never mind, it is not important. All that is important is that you are here now".

One day when Timothy was 14 Mammy, who was the large Negro woman who was in charge of the kitchen for the main house, took him aside and told him his background. "Child, your pappy and mammy died of some horrible sickness on the ship on the way to Charlestown, you was only about 10-12 months old when you arrived in Charlestown. The way I heared it two of the women on the ship took turns feeding you to keep you alive. Your parents were to come here as indentured servants for Mistah Thomas. That means they was each to work for Mistah Thomas for six years to pay for their passage, then they be free folk.

Missus Martha had just had her second baby born dead. So she took you and pretended to be your mama and she named you 'Timothy' after her daddy. No one knows what your parents named you. She died when you was about four-year-old and Mistah Thomas didn't want you livin' in the big house no more, so he had you go live with the slaves.

You always likes to run and as you know you is the fastest runner round here. Mistah Thomas has made a powerful mount of money bettin' on your running.

The Cherokee injuns who comes here for trading even had some of their fastest men run against you and you beat 'um all. That's when the Cherokee named you 'nu-da da-tsi-da-hi-', which mean 'Crazy Runner' because you don't slow down for anything. It kinda stuck amongst the injuns and some tother plantation owners and thats is all I knows about cha."

He thought about that for quite a while and finally decided that since he did not have a real "white man's" name that he had been given when he was born and "Crazy Runner" seemed to fit; he would make that his name. He did like to run and had always enjoyed the feeling of the wind rushing through his hair. Some races were short, maybe 50 yards. When he raced the injuns he would always run through thick forests and sometimes for as long as five miles. For him running that distance was easy and he only got winded if he was racing uphill for more than a mile.

The Cherokee who frequently came to the plantation to trade had taught him how to throw a knife and how to make and shoot a bow and arrow. Mr. Cook had bought a knife from the Cherokee and gave it to him as a present for winning a race. It had a nice wood handle, was about ten inches long, and sharp on both sides.

Because of the hunting trips with Mr. Cook he had become very good at tracking all types of game.

He had been taught to read and write and do his numbers by the overseer's wife.

His daily life, when he wasn't hunting or running, was composed of working in the fields with the Negro slaves.

CHAPTER 2—RUNNING AWAY

It was April of 1750 and Crazy Runner had just turned 17 years old the month before. Since they did not know what his birthday was, Mrs. Cook had given him the same birthday she had, March 17, Saint Patrick's Day.

He had told Mr. Cook that he would like to leave. Mr. Cook said no. According to Mr. Cook's logic, his mother and father each owed him six years of labor, which meant that he needed to pay his parents debt that totaled twelve years of labor. He had not really been able to do much work until about eight years old so, according to Mr. Cook's logic that meant that he owed three more years of labor.

By Crazy Runner's logic, the money he had earned from his running for Mr. Cook should have more than equaled three years of labor. Therefore, on a beautiful April morning, he left with nothing more than the clothes on his back, his knife, and a small package of food Mammy had made for him. The Negros covered for him, so it was three days before Mr. Cook had any idea that he was gone.

CRAZY RUNNER - TRAILBLAZER - 1750

Crazy Runner headed northwest. He had really liked that area when he had gone hunting in that direction with Mr. Cook. Mr. Cook had told him there were mountains in that direction and he had never seen a mountain. Beginning on the third day, he was in unfamiliar territory.

Most 17-year-olds would have probably panicked at being in a strange place, all alone, and having to fend for himself. Not only did he quickly get used to this, but he liked it.

On the fourth day, he made himself a bow and six arrows for hunting. On the fifth day, he tried several times to kill rabbits, squirrels, deer, and a fox with the bow and arrow, but he was not yet a good enough shot. He came to a small river that had fish in it. He was able to get a fish by stabbing it with one of his arrows. As he pulled the fish out of the water, he looked up to see two Cherokee braves looking at him and laughing. He thought, "Let them laugh, at least I am going to eat". They went on their way and he fixed his meal.

He stayed in that area working on shooting his bow and arrow. It took several days, but he got to the point that finally he could hit a rabbit about fifteen feet away.

At that point, he started moving northwest again. The woods were very dense in this area. It was evident that no groups of white men had traveled in this direction, because there were no worn trails with wagon ruts. He found several worn trails, some were from animals and some were from the Cherokee who would travel to the white man's villages to the east, northeast and southeast for trading.

Whenever possible he would try to find a place to camp where he could see the stars at night. He once stopped for several days after he had killed a deer. He had carefully bled it as Mr. Cook had taught him, then he cut out the innards, and let the skin stretch and dry in a place where there was sun and the wind was blowing. He knew that in the towns, they paid good money for animal pelts and he had observed that the Cherokee had made their clothes from animal skins. When the skin was good and dry he used it for a pack to hold his arrows and food. Then he continued traveling northwest. Last year he remembered some English-speaking Cherokee told him that there was a sacred place and mountains in this direction.

His inquisitiveness urged him on.

Chapter 3—Kituhwa

Crazy Runner was quickly adapting to the outdoor life. It had only been a couple of weeks, but he felt at ease and that this was where he belonged. He was not sure what he was looking for, or if he was looking for anything. He just liked being outdoors. He was happier than he ever remembered being.

One morning as he was walking, he recognized a noise and quickly ducked. An arrow hit the tree next to him. He turned and saw three Cherokee braves starting toward him from about twenty feet away. He quickly pulled the arrow from the tree and took off running.

As he was running, he wondered why the Cherokee were trying to kill him. As long as he could remember, the Cherokee had always been very peaceful and friendly to whites.

He kept getting farther and farther ahead of them. After about one mile, he already had a 50-foot lead and one of the braves stopped. A second brave stopped after about three miles when he had about a 100-foot lead. The third brave stopped when he had about a 200-foot lead and they had gone about four miles. He continued running for about another ½ mile and then slowed to a walk.

The terrain he was in was rocky with many pine needles on the ground. The bottoms of his feet were slightly bleeding. He simply was not used to running in this type of terrain. He came upon a stream and soaked his feet, while he cut up the deerskin to make moccasins and leggins for himself and a quiver for his arrows. He cut long thin strips to use for binding. He made a place in his right leggin that would hold his knife.

Then he looked at the arrow he had taken from the tree. This was not like the arrows he had or the ones he had seen the Cherokees making when they visited the plantation. This arrow had more feathers and instead of a wooden carved tip, it had a small piece of rock, which had been sharpened to a point and was tied to the tip of the arrow. He reasoned that the extra feathers must have something to do with the extra weight of the stone point. Crazy Runner thought that the reason for this type of point was to do more damage when it hit the animal being hunted.

He looked around the bottom of the stream and found several stones about the same size as the one used for the arrow tip. He put them into his quiver and decided to continue walking.

He came to an open area and could see a ridge with a tall tree on top. He decided to climb that tree and see where he was and what was around him.

After he got as far up the tree as he dared climb he beheld the most beautiful sight he had ever seen. Off to the northwest was land that seemed to reach up to the sky. He reasoned that must be what they call a mountain. He also saw a very large waterfall that looked to only be a few miles away. This area had a lot of hills and valleys. He saw a ridge to his left that seemed to lead in the direction of the waterfall. It seemed to him that it would be foolish to travel up and down hills when he could walk along that ridge and get most of the way there.

After walking for about an hour and a half along the ridge, he could see the entire waterfall. At the bottom of the waterfall appeared to be a town. He headed for the town. He had gotten to within a mile of the town when he realized it was a Cherokee village. He had been told that the Indians lived in tepees so they could move around a lot. However, this village consisted of houses built of wood and stone, almost the same as a white man might build.

He reasoned that all of the Cherokee he had known were peaceful, except for the three who had shot at him earlier today. Perhaps they had simply mistaken him for someone else and he calmly walked into the village. There was some type of yell and he was surrounded by many braves with knives out and arrows about to shoot him.

Crazy Runner immediately placed his bow, arrows, and knife on the ground and stepped away from them. He had learned some Cherokee so he pointed to himself and said, "nu-da da-tsi-da-hi—do-hi", which he hoped meant "Crazy Runner peaceful".

They lead him to a building, pushed him through the door and then closed the door. This building had one small room with no windows and nothing inside. After about an hour, an old Cherokee brave came in and lead Crazy Runner to a circle of men. The old brave said, in good English, "What is your name?"

"Crazy Runner."

"What is your white man name?" he asked.

"I don't have one."

"Why are you here?"

"I ran away from the plantation where I was a slave."

The old brave explained this to the men in the circle. The three young braves who had chased him this morning appeared and evidently told the men in the circle about their earlier encounter with him. Another brave spoke up and said something. Crazy Runner recognized him has one of the braves who had laughed at him when he caught his first fish. The men in the circle laughed.

The old man said, "This is a sacred place to the Cherokee. No white man has been here before and lived. We will put you through some tests to tell us whether you are worthy of being a friend to the Cherokee. You are just to stay around the village today and tonight you will be locked in that room for the night. Tomorrow you will start your tests."

As he walked around, he noticed some people taking stones like the ones he had found and they were sharpening them on some large rocks. Now he knew how they got the sharp points.

As a foolish young man he had no fear, Crazy Runner was not afraid for he believed he was invincible. Later in life when he looked back on this moment he could not believe he had been so reckless, but glad he had been.

Chapter 4—The Tests

The next morning he was not well rested. During the night, he started worrying about what type of tests he might be asked to perform. He really had no concept and many uncomfortable thoughts kept entering his head. Later he would find out that was part of the test.

The old brave came, took the bar off the door, let him out and once again he was taken to the circle of men. He was told the first test was to be a race. As soon as this was said, he smiled. Because no one was a fast as he was.

Four braves went with him and they climbed up the side of the waterfall to near the top. They lead him along the edge of the river for about two miles and then they headed into the woods. As they traveled along one of the braves would stop about every mile. They followed a trail for two miles when they came to a cave. Now there was only one brave left with him. The brave told him that he was to stand in front of the entrance of the cave and that there was a bear in the cave. The brave drew one line in the ground about five feet from the cave entrance. He drew a second line in the ground about twenty-five feet from the entrance. Crazy Runner was to stand on the second line. Crazy Runner was to yell loudly and when the bear came out and reached the first line, then he could start running and must reach the top of the waterfalls before the bear caught him.

The brave then climbed up to the top of the entrance of the cave and leaning over proceeded to throw stones into the cave and yell as Crazy Runner was also yelling. It only took about three minutes before the bear appeared at the entrance of the cave. Crazy Runner immediately started yelling and jumping around. When the bear started after him then he started running. However, Crazy Runner did not follow the trail they had taken to get to the cave, because the instructions only said get to the top of the waterfall. Instead, he figured to head for the top of the waterfalls by the most direct route, which was through some dense woods and where there was no trail. The bear only traveled for about 50 yards and the woods were so dense that the bear had too much trouble navigating so the bear stopped following Crazy Runner. When he saw that the bear was no longer chasing him, Crazy Runner started walking to the top of the waterfalls.

The brave who had first agitated the bear had climbed down and was headed down the trail when the bear, who had given up on Crazy Runner, started after him. Since this brave knew the area, he was able to climb some rocks and get away in another direction. Because Crazy Runner had not followed the trail, none of the other three braves knew what was going on and they were just waiting. When Crazy Runner got to the top of the waterfalls, he climbed down to the village.

The old brave asked what had happened to the other braves. Crazy Runner said, "After I started running I never saw them".

CRAZY RUNNER - TRAILBLAZER - 1750

About a half-hour later, the four braves came back to camp and told the men in the circle what had happened.

The old brave told Crazy Runner, "You have passed the first test. It is now time for your second test."

Two braves were brought to stand in front of him. The old brave stood between them and said, "This is a test of justice and balance in the world. This brave (indicating the one on his right) has killed the wife of this brave (pointing to the one on his left). What should the punishment be?"

When the overseer's wife had taught him to read, much of the reading was from the Bible. One passage immediately came to Crazy Runner, "An eye for an eye". Crazy Runner said, "That brave (pointing to the one with the dead wife) should be allowed to kill the wife of the other brave."

The old brave repeated the answer to the men in the circle as the two braves left. The men in the circle all nodded. The old brave said, "That is what Cherokee justice and balance are about. You have passed this test. The last test is to prove your worth to the tribe. You are to take the weapons you brought with you and kill a deer, rabbit, fox, and squirrel. You are to have all three lying in this circle before the sun is straight up tomorrow."

Crazy Runner looked around and decided that his best chance would be in the area to the east. He took off running hard. He thought that no animals would be within a mile of the village because of all of the noise. He ran about a mile and then started looking for tracks. It did not take long before he spotted a squirrel in a tree and killed it. He also got a rabbit. He knew his best chance to kill a deer would be in the very early morning. He could not find any fox tracks in this area, in fact he could not remember seeing any fox tracks for the last two days. Just before dark, he did spot a deer and was able to kill it.

Putting the deer over his shoulders and with the rabbit in one hand and the squirrel in the other he ran back to the camp and deposited all three in the circle. Then he took off running northeast, since he had already been to the southeast and east without seeing any fox tracks. He was happy that there was a bright moon so he could still run, only having to slow down occasionally when the thick trees blocked out the moonlight.

He found a place by a stream to rest and waited for daylight. As soon as the sky started to lighten, but even before the sun was visible, he started looking for fox tracks. It took almost an hour but he found them and tracked him a short distance to a den. He stuck the arrow with the rock point in softly and felt something and it moved. He quickly thrust the arrow in more and heard a squeal. He slowly pulled the arrow out and there was a fox dying on the other end of the arrow. He picked up the fox by the neck and started his run back. By the time he reached the village the sun was not far above the horizon. He had accomplished his final test.

The old brave told him, "You now are considered to be a friend of the Cherokee and a Cherokee brave. As long as you follow our ways, you are welcome in Kituhwa." That is when he found out that the old braves name was "yo-nv—a-di-si" or Running Bear.

Running Bear told him, "Whenever you are around Cherokee just say "tsa-la-gi tsu-li-tsv-ya-s-di, which means "Cherokee brave and you will not be harmed.

"What is the difference between a brave and a warrior?" Crazy Runner asked.

"A brave is any man who is old enough to hunt, go into battle, and understands the ways of the Cherokee. A warrior is a brave who has honored the tribe when he was in battle."

Chapter 5—Rifle

Over the next several weeks, Crazy Runner had learned many things. He had learned that while his bow was good, it was not strong enough to be able to kill large animals. He was shown a tree of stronger wood and used that to make a new bow. He also was given better material for a bowstring. He had made a dozen arrows with sharp rock points.

He had learned about hand-to-hand fighting Indian style. He was taught how to use a knife properly in a fight.

The Cherokee did not have many horses, but he was shown how to ride a horse.

Running Bear had been his mentor for all of this training and told him that he was now ready for battle, should the need arise.

Crazy Runner already knew how to track animals, but he learned how to set traps for small game. He had gathered several pelts during his hunting and collected enough to trade for a rifle.

His knowledge of the Cherokee language was growing every day. The members of the tribe all helped him learn new words, while occasionally laughing when he would mispronounce one.

Crazy Runner went with Running Bear and a group who were going to trade with the white men to the east. Since this was not the direction of the Violet Plantation Crazy Runner went with them, taking all of his pelts.

When the white men at the trading post saw Crazy Runner with the Cherokee, they asked many questions. Crazy Runner knew that to the Cherokee lying was very bad. Therefore, he answered truthfully all of the questions they asked, but just not the complete truth. When he was asked why he was living with the Cherokee, he answered that his parents were dead from sickness and he had found the Cherokee to be very hospitable people—both of which were true.

He found out that it was the last week of May, which meant he had left the Violet Plantation about seven weeks ago. In Crazy Runner's mind he had only been gone about two weeks, time had indeed passed very fast.

Crazy Runner overheard some of the white men whispering that it was not going to be as easy to take advantage of the Indians with this white man with them. Crazy Runner whispered that to the Cherokee.

Crazy Runner did some hard bargaining to get a 50-caliber Pennsylvania rifle with a 46" barrel, pistol, shot, wading, and a full powder horn in exchange for his pelts. He was happy in that he now had a rifle, which was much better for hunting bear than arrows.

When the Cherokee would wonder if a deal was good or not they would look at Crazy Runner and he would nod yes or no. This surprised Crazy Runner until he realized that the Cherokee had no knowledge of the worth of their pelts. They only killed animals for food and clothing, certainly not for sport and definitely not for money. No one really took advantage of anyone and both sides ended up getting what they wanted;

although the owners of the trading post were not happy that they had not been able to make as many trades that were very good for them as they had previously.

When they got back to camp, he spent several days teaching the members of the tribe who had rifles the best way to aim them for accuracy at distances and how to change the load to match the distance they wanted to fire.

Because of this trading trip and his knowledge of rifles, Crazy Runner now had an exalted place in the tribe.

Chapter 6—Exploring

Crazy Runner decided to do some exploring on his own and ten days after the trading post trip he headed northwest into the mountains. He said good-bye to Running Bear saying that he wanted to see the country and would be back sometime. Running Bear warned him to beware of the Shawnee, Creek tribes to the north and west and the Chickasaw tribe to the southwest. The Cherokee had been warring with these tribes for many years and if they found out he was a friend of the Cherokee they would kill him.

He loved being up high and being able to see for many miles, although all he could see most of the time were treetops. After climbing to the top of this mountain range, he traveled along the tops of the mountains in a northerly direction for several days. Then he went down the west side of the mountains, wandered around the land learning landmarks, location of water and animals. What amazed him most was how dense the forest was. At many places, the trees were so thick he could not even see the sky. When he would come to open areas, he was even more surprised by the scenes that unfolded before him.

He found several more Cherokee villages during this time. The Cherokee were a very close-knit people. The Cherokee villages were permanently placed in locations close to water and it was only a one-day walk from one village to another, if one were to follow the trails.

Crazy Runner did not like walking as much as he liked running. Therefore, he would usually jog or run for many miles at a time. He found if he stayed on the paths he could get from one village through a second and arrive at a third at the end of one day.

Staying on the trails was not what he wanted to do. He wanted to make his own trails. He found himself wondering, as he traveled, how many white men had seen what he was beholding now. It really excited him to think that he might be the first white man ever to have seen some of these places.

He had no trouble finding game to eat. He would usually kill them with his bow and arrow since he wanted to save his gunpowder for big animals. He had seen tracks of bears, but had not seen one. If he did see a bear, he wanted it to be at a distance or in a location favorable to him.

He found many waterfalls, lakes, rivers, and mountains. Most of the area in which he was traveling was not flat, but contained many hills and valleys. The hills were not mountains, like back to the east near Kituhwa. Whenever possible he would camp for the night in a location where he could see the stars.

He did occasionally see Indians who were not Cherokee, but it was always at a distance and as far as he could tell they did not see him. He did not go out of his way to visit Indians, especially after what Running Bear had told him about the Shawnee, Creek, and Chickasaw; he was interested in seeing the country.

Several times, he would travel in a large circle around a particularly nice area. He was thankful that he always recognized the area when he completed his circle. Running Bear had told him that being able to recognize places you had previously been was one way to make sure the spirits were with you.

Chapter 7—A Bear

One piece of advice given him by Running Bear was not to be around tall trees when there was lightning. Crazy Runner had noticed that a very large storm with a lot of thunder and lightning was headed his way. He remembered that once before he was in this exact area, he had found a nice cave and that cave would be a good place to wait out this storm.

He checked out the cave and found signs of animals, but there were none there now. He gathered firewood and put it in the cave. The cave was only about twenty feet deep and twenty feet wide, but it was very tall so the smoke from the fire would go either up or out the opening and not bother him. Then he killed a rabbit. He had just made it back into the cave when the storm reached this area. There was a lot of lightning and thunder.

He made a nice fire and cooked the rabbit. Since it was late in the afternoon, he decided to just relax and let the storm pass and he would go out the next morning. His stomach was full and he found a nice soft place at the back of the cave to sleep.

He was not sure how long he had been asleep when there was a slight noise. He awoke to find a large bear about ten feet from him, he was glad he was a light sleeper. When Crazy Runner moved the bear stood on his hind feet and began growling at him. The bear, while standing on his hind feet, was the same height as he was, but easily outweighed Crazy Runner by at least 300 pounds. The major problem for Crazy Runner was that the bear was between his weapons and him. The only weapon he had was his knife. He knew the knife was sharp, because before he went to sleep he had sharpened it on a rock he found in the cave.

Crazy Runner quickly assessed his situation. There was about ten feet of space to both the left and right of the bear. He knew the bear was not as agile or fast when standing on his rear feet. His weapons were located to the right and about five feet behind the bear. Just because something like this might happen, he had the rifle ready to fire. All he had to do was reach it.

He danced first to the left and then the right to see the reaction of the bear. The bear did not move to either side. That led him to believe that perhaps this was an older bear and moved very slowly. He quickly started to run to the bear's right directly toward his weapons. The bear stretched out a paw and caught Crazy Runner on top of his left shoulder tearing the flesh as we went down on all fours blocking Crazy Runner's path.

Crazy Runner jumped back to where he had been and the bear again went to a full upright position. He picked up a small rock and threw it at the face of the bear. It caught the bear on the nose and did not seem to do anything except make it madder.

Crazy Runner picked up a larger rock and with all of his might threw it at the bear's neck and at the same time started running to the left of the bear. The large rock hit its mark and stunning the bear and knocking it back a couple of steps so the bear was directly between where Crazy Runner was headed and his weapons.

He picked up another rock and again threw it as hard as possible at the bear's neck and at the same time charged directly at the bear thrusting his knife into the neck of the bear. Blood started spurting out of the bear's neck. As soon as the plunged the knife in he immediately pulled it out and jumped back just in time to be missed by both claws coming at him. Now the bear was not protecting his perceived property, the cave, he was fighting for his life. That made him even more dangerous.

Crazy Runner knew that now that the bear was injured he would become more aggressive. The bear got down on all fours and slowly started toward Crazy Runner. This time Crazy Runner's rock caught the bear in the left eye and blood started spurting from that eye. The bear stopped in his tracks.

While he was stopped Crazy Runner took his knife and threw it will all of his strength. It sunk deep into the bear's right eye. The bear immediately let out a horrifying scream and dropped to the ground.

Crazy Runner ran and jumped over the top of the bear toward his weapons. The moaning screaming bear was clawing at the knife in his eye. Crazy Runner took his bow and arrow and placed two arrows into the bear's heart. It did not take the bear long to die.

Despite the storm, he went to a nearby stream and lay in it soaking the wound to his left shoulder. He took some tree moss and mud and held it to the wound as he walked back to the cave.

He had just killed his first bear without the aid of his rifle or pistol. According to what Running Bear had told him, this made him a brave to be looked up to by the Cherokee.

Crazy Runner carefully skinned the bear. It took three days for the pelt to dry. He had also cooked most of the meat in the fire to take with him so he would not have to stop to find food for many days. Running Bear had told him to always use as much as possible of everything you kill. Unfortunately, because he was not close to a Cherokee village he was going to have to leave part of this bear for scavengers. He took the parts he was not using outside of the cave and spread them around.

Using the bear pelt, he made a large pouch he could put over his shoulders in which to carry the meat he had cooked. However, it took about a week before his left shoulder was healed enough to be able to carry it on both shoulders without pain.

Chapter 8—White Men

Several days after he had left the cave he came upon the tracks of some white men. They were easy to tell because they wore boots and Indians either wore moccasins or went barefoot. He was heading west and they were heading north. There were three of them and apparently, they were walking and taking their time. Evidently, they were not in as much of hurry to see the country as Crazy Runner.

The tracks were about one day old. He decided to follow these white men to see what they were doing. He was hoping they would be friendly and he would have someone to whom he could talk. He calculated that had not spoken to another person for over a month. Until he found these tracks and thought about it, he had not realized he missed talking English. The last time he had talked much English was at the trading post almost two months earlier.

The white men were following an animal trail. He stayed to the east of the animal trail about twenty feet and jogged along. At dusk, he could see a campfire not far ahead. It was a large fire. Crazy Runner thought it odd that these men would build such a large fire. Crazy Runner was fairly certain that he was in Creek territory, who were hereditary enemies of the Cherokee.

Slowly, Crazy Runner approached the fire staying in the darkness and careful to be very quiet. He completely circled the camp. He could see and hear the white men. They were not speaking English. One of Mr. Cook's visitors had sounded like that and he remembered Mr. Cook saying he was French. He wondered what Frenchmen were doing in Creek territory.

Crazy Runner decided that he would enter the camp. He carefully hid his bow and arrows, which were the only items he had that showed any relationship to the Cherokee. He slowly approached the camp being very careful not to make a sound. When he was about six feet from the campfire, he stepped out from behind a tree and said, "Hello".

The three men were completely startled by his presence. Since both of Crazy Runner's arms were resting on the barrel of his rifle, he did not appear to be a threat. The three men started talking in French. One of them said, "Welcome".

Crazy Runner said, "I saw your fire from quite aways off. I thought this must be an entire Creek village by the size of the fire."

In broken English the man said, "You trade with the Creek?"

"No, I am just hunting and trapping. When I get about all the pelts I can carry I go back to civilization, trade for supplies, and then start all over."

"Where you trade?"

"Carolinas."

"You should trade at Fort Toulouse. It is closer than the Carolinas, only ten days to the south and no mountains to cross."

Crazy Runner said, "Do you mind if I bed down with you tonight?"

"Come" and he pointed to a place where Crazy Runner could bed down. "What type of pelts do you have?"

"I've got a lot of fox and rabbit with a few beaver and deer."

"What about bear" said the man pointing to his pack?

"Only this one. I almost got killed getting him," he said laughing.

His laughter relaxed the men. Then Crazy Runner asked, "What are you hunting?"

"We are looking to set up trade agreements with the Indians."

"I guess that is the reason for the big fire, instead of you finding them, they will find you."

"Oui."

It was obvious that these men did not spend a lot of time out in the woods because they did not hear the Indians who were surrounding them at this moment as he did. "Well," Crazy Runner said, "You might want to act real friendly. Your trading partners are all around us."

With that, the man who had been doing the talking stood up and said something in French with a big smile.

Eight Creek stepped into the camp. They slowly looked around at each of the men. Crazy Runner was trying as best as he could to do nothing that would call attention to himself.

One of the Creek and the talkative man talked in French. After several minutes, the Indian pointed to Crazy Runner and said something that made the Frenchman laugh.

Crazy Runner asked, "What is so funny?"

He said, "They call you 'one who always runs'."

"That's me," was Crazy Runner's reply. He now knew that he had not been invisible to the Indians. He reasoned that they thought he was no threat to them so they did not bother him. Perhaps always running everywhere was not such a good idea. When he was running, he could not be as careful and not quite as observant as when he was walking.

After about thirty minutes, the Creek left.

Crazy Runner asked, "Are you going to get their pelts?"

"Oui."

With the business concluded, the four of them went to sleep.

The next morning the talkative Frenchman said, "I told you last night that it took ten days to reach Fort Toulouse, but if you run everywhere it might only take you five days." Everyone laughed and then broke camp. The Frenchmen headed back south and Crazy Runner headed west.

Chapter 9—Change

The Creek had headed east and the Frenchmen had headed south. Therefore, Crazy Runner decided to continue west after he had recovered his bow and arrows.

As was his habit, he started running immediately. After about thirty minutes, he stopped and started walking. He was thinking about the Creek and their name for him (one who always runs). To give him a name meant they had seen him more than once. Running Bear had told him that the Creek and Cherokee were mortal enemies and had warred many times over the years. The Cherokee had won most of these wars. According to Running Bear the Cherokee fought harder than the Creek because the Cherokee were a stationary people, their villages were permanent and sacred to them, while the Creek would move their villages periodically. When an enemy attacks your permanent home, you fight much harder to protect it.

If the Creek were to capture Crazy Runner and find out he had ties to the Cherokee it would mean a slow and very painful death for him. So far, they had thought he was harmless so they had not bothered him. If he were to continue running, the Creek might not bother him at all. However, he thought he was also close to Shawnee and Chickasaw territory, two other hereditary tribal enemies of the Cherokee.

Therefore, Crazy Runner decided it would be safer to walk instead of run most of the time. However, he decided he would run whenever he came to open areas. Not because he was in a hurry to get out of the open areas, but because since anyone could already see him anyway it should not make any difference at all. It would also allow him to keep in good running shape.

Whenever possible he tried to stay at the tops of hills, because it took less effort and time. Occasionally he would see something interesting in a valley and travel down to investigate. While traveling along the ridge tops he would stay in the trees and if it were open, he would travel just below the top so he would not attract unwanted attention.

He marveled at all he saw. The scenery was marvelous. Except for the Frenchmen, it had been months since he had seen any white men. It amazed him that he was seeing what other white men had not seen.

He kept traveling west and after many days came to a very wide river. This must be what the Cherokee call "u'-ta-na' yv-wi gv-nah-i-ta" (Big River). He liked looking at it and listening to it. He spent two nights and one day by it just marveling at how large it was and how the sounds were so much different from what he had previously heard rivers make.

When he decided to leave, he headed northeast, which was an area that would be new to him.

Chapter 10—Shawnee

Crazy Runner had traveled northeast for a week in new country. He was extremely observant and noticed how each day the scenery changed. Yes, there were many trees everywhere, but the trees were all different. Some types of trees he knew the names of and some he did not. He thought that it was all beautiful and he loved every moment of it.

On the eighth day after leaving the Big River, from the top of a hill, he spotted a large Shawnee village. This village was located on the shore of another big river. This river was almost as wide as the first one he had seen. To be on the safe side he decided to back track and give this large village a wide berth.

As he headed down the same trail he had come up, he suddenly stopped realizing that the animals he had heard when he first passed over this trail less than a hour ago were no longer scurrying around. That meant there was something in the area that had scared them. Crazy Runner slowly moved off the trail, moving very cautiously, and listening intently. He heard a twig snap about ten yards behind him and at almost the same time heard another twig snap about twenty yards to his right.

Immediately he grabbed a good hold on his things and took off running. He had not made but about three or four steps when he heard the yelling of Indians on his trail. With quick looks over his shoulder, he saw at least four braves and assumed they were from the large Shawnee village.

Crazy Runner was easily outdistancing the braves. Because he was tall and had long legs, he could easily jump over bushes that were three feet tall in full stride. He was in the lead so he chose to run in the thick brush where he could use his jumping ability to get an even greater gap between himself and his pursuers.

After about an hour, they were no longer following him. He was not positive, but he felt he had at least a 500-yard advantage on them. He slowed to a walk while carefully listening.

He then spotted another group of braves to his right heading toward him. It could not be the same group he had previously outrun and it appeared they had not seen him. Slowly, he moved further ahead looking for a place to conceal himself while they passed.

Then he noticed a third group heading directly toward him from the direction in which he was headed. The group in front of him had at least five braves, the group behind him had at least four braves, and the group now to his right, had at least four braves. There was no way he could fight them and he could find no place for concealment, so he had to run for it. He calculated that the direction he was about to start running was directly toward the Shawnee camp. He simply hoped he could find a place to hide or a way to get past the village before he got too close to it.

As soon as he started running, the Indians all started yelling.

Now he heard the yelling to his left also. They had him boxed in. They were to his left, right and behind him. He wondered if they were purposefully hunting him since there were so many in one area. His only hope was to outrun them quickly in hopes of changing his direction after he outdistanced them.

Based on the sounds of their yelling he knew he had the biggest lead on the ones to his left that he had already outrun. He thought they must be tired. He crossed the top of the hill and could see the village directly in front of him about one mile away. He started to his left cutting in front of the ones on that side. From the sounds of their yelling, he knew he had gotten past the direction in which they were heading. He found some thick brush to hide in before any of the Indians crossed the ridge. He dove into the brush and lay as still as he could. All of the braves from all three groups were standing on top of the hill and looking around for him. Now that they were out in the open, he counted a total of 17. He was breathing heavy, but not as heavily as the braves were. He wanted to laugh, but was smart enough not to.

The braves split up into five smaller groups. One brave headed at a full run directly toward the village. The other four groups of four divided the directions they took. One group went along the ridge away from Crazy Runner. A second group came along the ridge directly above him. A third group was angling down the hill away from him. The last group was angling down the hill directly toward him.

If he waited until they were close that meant the other eight would be at a greater distance and he would only have to outrun eight of them. It seemed that he was going to be caught in the middle of them if he did not start running; however, this brush was very thick and the chances of him being seen were very slim.

Suddenly, he heard screams coming from directly behind him. There were four women with baskets, who must have been picking berries, and they were pointing directly at him. He stood and started to run, but he was immediately surrounded.

He carefully and slowly stepped out into the open and laid down his rifle, pistol, bow, arrows, knife, and pack. His hands were tied behind him and he was taken to the village.

Chapter 11—The Village

Crazy Runner was tied to a stake in the center of the village. He had no idea why they had done this. This was nothing like the justice of the white man or the Cherokee.

He spent the rest of the day and all night tied to that post with no one approaching him at all. The next morning one brave walked up to him and said something that he thought sounded French. Crazy Runner just shrugged his shoulders and the brave walked away.

About noon, a group of braves came into the camp. One of them walked up to him and said, "English".

"Yes."

"How are you called?"

Crazy Runner said, "The Cherokee call me 'Crazy Runner' and the Creek call me 'One who always runs'."

The brave laughed and then said, "Why are you in our country?"

"I was a white man's slave. I ran away. I like seeing new places so I have just kept traveling gathering pelts for trading."

The brave asked, "How did you know what the Cherokee and Creek call you?"

Crazy Runner answered, "When I was a slave I would run many races against the Cherokee and always win. That is how they gave me that name. Several days ago, I came upon some French traders who were meeting with the Creek. One of the Frenchmen also spoke English and told me what the Creeks called me."

"From what I have been told the Cherokee name fits you best. My name is 'mkateewa mhweewa', which means Black Wolf."

"Why were the Shawnee coming after me?" Crazy Runner asked.

"They were not after you. They were simply three different scouting groups. We are at war with the Creek so we send out scouting groups every day searching for their raiding parties. When the first group came across your trail, they thought you were a Creek scout, but they could never get close enough to you to find out you were a white man."

Now Crazy Runner laughed. Then he asked, "What is going to happen to me now?"

The tribal elders are discussing that now and he left. He motioned to a squaw and she came and gave Crazy Runner some water.

About an hour later, Black Wolf came back and told him that the elders had made a decision. It seems that some of the braves felt embarrassed at being outrun by a white man. They want to see if you can stand up to a warrior's test.

Crazy Runner immediately thought of the three Cherokee tests and without hesitation said, "Alright".

Black Wolf said, "You are either very brave or very foolish to say yes without knowing what the test is to be."

CRAZY RUNNER - TRAILBLAZER - 1750

Now Crazy Runner was not sure of what he had gotten himself into. He suddenly thought that the Shawnee test might be different from those of the Cherokee. As the brave was untying him, he asked, "What must I do?"

"You must run the gauntlet."

"What does that mean?"

"You take off your shirt and then you run through a row of braves on each side who will be hitting you with sticks. If you make it through without passing out or dying then you will be considered as brave as a Shawnee warrior."

Crazy Runner thought to himself, that he had to slow down and start asking questions before agreeing to things.

There were two lines drawn in the dirt about eight feet apart. Braves were lining up in a straight line along each line. Each had a stick about three feet long. There were ten braves on each side. He was told that each brave could not cross the line in front of him. Crazy Runner must stay between the two lines and must reach the chief at the far end, about thirty feet away from the starting line, before he is considered to have passed the test.

Crazy Runner looked at the twenty braves and several of them he recognized as ones he had outrun yesterday. They had a grudge against him so they would be swinging extra hard. He calculated that if he stayed close to the braves on one side that would mean that only half of them would be able to hit him. In addition, if he were real close to them they would not be able to get in a full swing.

He was about ten feet from the starting line and figured that if he started running from here he would be at full speed by the time he reached the line. Crazy Runner took off heading directly toward the middle of the space between the two lines. As soon as he reached the starting line, he immediately moved to the far right of the space between the lines so he was about one foot from the right line. This shocked the first and second warriors because it looked as though he was headed directly toward them. They tried to swing while backing up and barely touched him. The third and fourth warriors were quick and got in a good swing but it was only a glancing blow off his back. The fifth warrior did not try to swing down, but instead swung up to try to knock Crazy Runner off his feet. Due to his speed and the blow glancing off his forearm, it did not have the desired effect. The sixth warrior did get in a good blow to his right arm, which slightly threw him off balance and into the center of the path. One warrior on the left got in a blow to his back, which made a cut. It only took Crazy Runner two steps to be back to speed and back to the right side. Evidently, the seventh warrior thought that he was going over to the other side and so he was not prepared to swing as Crazy Runner ran by. The eighth warrior held his stick straight out with his body braced behind it. It was obvious that his purpose was to slow him down and push him more to the center. While the eighth warrior's feet were not over the line, much of his upper body was. Crazy Runner slammed his shoulder into the shoulder of the eighth warrior knocking him backward, which in turn knocked the ninth and tenth warriors off balance as Crazy Runner blew by them and up to the chief.

    The chief inspected him and found that Crazy Runner had two welts, one slight bleeding area and not much else. Crazy Runner had passed the test.

    It only took two days for his welts to heal to the point that wearing a shirt was comfortable. During those two days, he learned enough of the Shawnee language to get by.

    He was asked several more questions about the Frenchmen he had met. It seemed that the Shawnee were extremely interested and concerned that the Creeks were doing business with French.

Chapter 12—Creek

On the third day, in the early afternoon, he gathered his things and headed off to the east. He noticed that many of the Shawnee were watching him as he departed. He was not sure why, so he took off running. He ran up a hill in the open. When he glanced over his shoulder, he could see that no one in the village was following him, but many were still looking at him. He thought that perhaps they were just watching him run, so he kept to the open along the top of the ridge and even increased his running speed. As he finally went out of sight, he was wondering what the Shawnee were now calling him.

He had run for over a mile within sight of the village and continued running for another two miles before slowing down to a walk and enjoying the countryside which was new to him. He was walking along an animal path. He had walked about another two miles when he heard the sounds of many feet headed toward him.

He went back about ¼ mile to an area of very heavy brush. He climbed up a tree and could see many Indians still headed in this direction spread out so there was no way for him to go north, south or east. Those to the north and south could easily catch him if he tried running to the Shawnee village. He could tell they were Creeks, he could also tell that one was the Frenchman he had earlier met and talked with. He crawled out on a branch and dropped down in the middle of many heavy bushes, by doing it in this way he knew he would leave no sign of going into this cover. The space he was in was cramped for his size, but at least he was certain he was safe.

He only had to wait about fifteen minutes to have Creek braves wearing war paint surrounding him on every side. They were very quiet and were in many small groups of five or six, but each group stayed within sight of another group. Evidently, hand signals were being sent between groups. Many of them had rifles. They must have been given the signal to stop, because one group about ten feet west of him stopped at the same time that another group about thirty feet north of him stopped and a group about forty feet south of him also stopped. He was certain that there was another small group east of him. They had gotten off the animal trail and were sitting on the ground. All he could do was to sit quietly and wait for them to pass.

Crazy Runner thought that it was about four to five miles from here to the Shawnee camp. He thought that the Shawnee probably did not send out their daily scouting groups this far, so they probably had no idea that this many Creek were this close to them.

Even if he wanted to warn the Shawnee, he could not. He might be able to outrun the braves, but he could not outrun this many arrows or musket balls. All he could do was wait until they moved west toward the Shawnee camp and then he would move east.

He was surprised that as close as he was to them that he

heard no talking, not even whispering. After they sat down, he could no longer see them.

These were very disciplined braves. When he had first spotted the Creek, Crazy Runner thought that it was already late afternoon. Having to be still and quiet was not in his nature and he was getting anxious to move. However, he was intelligent enough to know that any movement could cost him his life.

Therefore, he needed to occupy his mind. He started remembering the land he had traveled over since he had left the Cherokee village. He was able to recall every stream, river and trail (human and animal). That kept him so occupied that he did not even notice that the sun had gone down.

The sound of a whippoorwill, which did not sound exactly like one, brought him back to the present. Suddenly the woods came alive as the Creek were on the move. They must have been planning a raid at dawn and were going to move ahead slowly to get in position before the sun came up.

The night was overcast and Crazy Runner could not see anything. That was helpful for the Creek and bad for him. That meant he did not dare leave his hiding place until daylight. He knew that getting out of this heavy brush would make a lot of noise and he could not take the chance that there might be a brave left behind to guard their rear, so he went to sleep.

When he awoke, the sun was already up. Slowly he stood up just high enough so he could see in each direction, without exposing his entire head. After looking in each direction for several minutes, he knelt down and with his knife hacked a way through the bushes. When he was finished, he stood up and surveyed the area in all directions as before. When he was again satisfied that no one was around he crawled out of his hiding place. Then he slowly made his way east making sure to stay off the animal trail he had been following.

After about two miles, he came to a river. He scouted around and found several braves guarding many canoes. He noticed that the braves were all standing in a circle talking. Two canoes were downstream of the others and hidden from the braves view by some thick bushes and a slight bend in the river. Crazy Runner crawled through the brush to the canoe furthest away from the braves. There was an oar in the bottom of the boat.

Crazy Runner had never been in a canoe. He had witnessed many others, mostly Indians, in canoes and observed how they controlled it. He placed his things on the bottom of the canoe in the center and carefully pushed the canoe slightly away from the shore.

He started walking in the water leading the canoe downstream. He was making sure he was staying close to the shoreline so the braves would not see him. There was another bend in the river about twenty feet away. When he had reached that bend, he carefully got into the canoe, on his knees straddling his things.

CHAPTER 13—RAPIDS

Crazy Runner carefully and slowly paddled the canoe downstream making sure he was as quiet as possible. He had learned while hunting that sounds travel farther on water. When he thought he had gone about a mile, he started speeding up his strokes. Then he would put the oar on one side and then the other side without stroking to practice steering the canoe.

He had traveled another mile or so staying close to the west shoreline when he saw a pack of wolves at the edge of the river. The leader of the wolves was a large white wolf. He steered the canoe to the center of the river with the wolves yapping at him from the shore. He kept watching them to see what they were doing, but evidently, they were smart enough to realize they could not travel as fast in the water as he could so they stayed on the shore.

Traveling downstream was very easy. If he wanted to speed up, all he had to do was paddle. If he just wanted the current to take him, with him just steering, he could do that also.

After another mile, the wolves were no longer visible from

the river. However, the Cherokee had taught him that you could never rely on wolves to do what you expect them to do.

Crazy Runner was thinking that this was not a bad way to travel. Just floating along and looking at the scenery. He decided to see how hard it was to go upstream and he turned the canoe around and started paddling. It was not hard, but it did take a lot more effort than going downstream. After a quarter-mile, he turned and started heading downstream again.

He knew that the Creek had arrived there by canoe. What he did not know was whether they had traveled upriver or downriver to get there.

He had spent enough time maneuvering the canoe to have confidence in his abilities to handle it should he see a Creek village. If he did come across the village the Creek had come from, there could not be many braves left there so that lessened his worry.

This river was heading south and that was the direction he was wanting to travel. He just floated along for the rest of the day. Near dark, he pulled in to a place on the east side of the river. He decided to pull the canoe completely out of the water and back into the brush so that it could not be seen from the river. If the Creek had traveled upstream then some of them might be coming by here on the river and he did not want to take a chance that they would see the canoe.

The next morning Crazy Runner went to the river to watch and listen for about ten minutes. Hearing nothing that sounded like paddling on the river he got out the canoe, loaded it up and headed downstream.

After several hours, he heard a noise coming from the direction in which he was headed. He could see that he was entering a canyon, so he reasoned that the noise was the echoing of the river within the canyon walls. As he continued, he noticed that the river was getting slightly narrower and running faster.

He stopped paddling and used the oar to both steer and slow down the canoe. He went around a bend and suddenly the river was very loud. There were rocks sticking up in the river and there was a lot of water that was white. He had heard about this, they were called rapids. There were few areas at the sides to land the canoe. The river was moving so fast the oar was no longer effective at slowing down the canoe.

Crazy Runner was also having to use the oar to push away from rocks the canoe was headed into. He tried to push the canoe toward the west shore, which was closest, by pushing off rocks in that direction, but the current always carried him back to the middle of the river. He then tried the same thing toward the east shore, with the same results.

He had four long strips tied around his waist that he used to hang up a deer to dry out after he killed it. As quickly as possible, he took his rifle, pistol, bow and quiver of arrows and put them in the bearskin. He wrapped one long strip around each end and tied it tightly. Then he took a third strip, tied the two ends together and put that third strip over his head.

Now he just had to find somewhere to get out of this water. He looked as far ahead as he could see and it seemed as though the river stopped. Then it came to him, it must be a waterfall!

He saw two large rocks close together. Each of these was about three feet above the water and several feet wide. He was able to maneuver the canoe between them where it stopped. The pressure of the water was so fierce that the canoe was starting to break up. Crazy Runner used the oar against the rock on the left to allow him to climb onto the rock on the right.

At the same time as his feet left the canoe, the canoe broke into pieces and continued downstream. Sitting on top of the rock, he was able to see the canoe go over the waterfall.

He analyzed his situation. The rock he was on was about ten feet from the west shore and about twenty feet from the east shore. There was one large rock, which was about halfway to the west shore. He knew he could leap far enough to reach that rock, but the sides were wet and smooth and he was not sure he would be able to hold on. Looking up he saw that the white wolf looking down at him from a ledge about twenty feet above the west shore.

Going toward the east shore there was one rock about two feet away. Downstream there was another large rock about three feet to the east and about three feet downstream. There was a third large rock about five feet east and about three feet downstream. Just past that rock was a large limb hanging just barely above the water. While it would be harder to get out of the river on the east side, there were no visible dangers on the east side so that was his safest route of escape.

He jumped to the close rock. When he got there, he was surprised to find a small ledge on the far side that he had previously not been able to see. By putting one foot on that ledge and the other behind him against the rock behind him, he was able to get enough of a push that the upper half of his body landed on top of the next rock, but he hit wrong and knocked the air out of himself.

He just hung there getting his wind back. After several minutes, he climbed on top of this rock. He would have to be careful because this rock was just about a foot above the water's surface and the top was wet and slick. He stopped for a minute to rest and looked around. As he was looking up the walls on the west side, he saw the entire pack of wolves looking down on him.

CRAZY RUNNER - TRAILBLAZER - 1750

This next jump was going to be tricky. He checked his pack to make sure that everything was still secure and it was. He could not jump directly for the rock, because much of his body would land in the water and the current would probably sweep him around the rock and over the waterfall. Therefore, he had to jump into the water just above the rock and let the current carry him to the rock. He did this and it worked as he had planned.

He rested a little on top of this rock while looking carefully at the tree limb. The tree limb was located about three feet directly downstream. The east shore was about four feet directly east. The tree limb appeared not very strong. He did not think it would hold the weight of both him and his pack.

He took off the pack and used the strip that had been around him and the fourth strip to tie the bundle together even more securely. He then got to a standing position and threw the pack to the shore with all of his might. It landed in a bush about a foot back from the water's edge. He then dove for the tree limb.

He caught the limb with his chest and quickly wrapped both arms around it. At the same moment, his body hit the limb he heard it crack. The limb broke free from the tree and went down in the water. Using the buoyancy of the limb and kicking for all he was worth, he was able to maneuver himself close enough to the shore where his feet touched bottom and he could crawl ashore.

He only rested for a minute and then went and retrieved his pack. After unpacking everything, he found that the rifle and pistol appeared fine, except that the powder was wet. The bow had broken in half. He threw the bow away and carefully bound everything again in the bear skin.

He only had about four feet of shoreline and then rock walls heading up. He knew he was very tired and so he found a place to spend the night and got some much needed sleep.

The next morning he carefully surveyed his best method out of the canyon. The climb was straight up and down here and downriver. His only hope was slowly climbing at an angle going upriver, the direction from which he had come. He made the climb without incident.

He made a camp near the river, but at the head of the canyon. It took him a day to find a good hickory tree for wood for another bow and another day to make a useable bow.

Chapter 14—Big Jim

He remembered Running Bear telling him that everything you experience has lessons. Learn from your mistakes so you do not repeat them. What he had learned from this experience was that if he was ever canoeing again and heard a loud noise to immediately head to the safest shore.

He traveled one more day upstream and began recognizing the country. He had been here a few weeks after leaving Kituhwa. He changed his direction to go east-northeast so he would be still experiencing new country.

He came to a gorge with a fast flowing river at the bottom. He could see rapids all along the gorge. This was like the river where he had encountered the rapids; only these rapids appeared much fiercer than the ones he had encountered. The difference was he could see no waterfalls. It appeared that the gorge started just a mile or so upstream. It looked as if he were to head north that he would come to a place to cross the river.

Actually, it was closer to two miles before he came to a place where the river was wide and deep enough so he could walk across with the water only up to his waist. He found a branch about six feet long lying on the ground. He cut off the little branches on it and he could use it to steady himself as he crossed the river. He bundled all of his things into the bearskin, put it over his shoulder and started across.

There was a strong current underneath the surface, but by taking small steps, he was able to get across the river. He found a nice place to camp beside the river and decided to camp there for the night. He was able to shoot several fish with a string tied to an arrow.

He saw a white man coming down the river in a canoe. Crazy Runner yelled to get his attention and then pointed downstream and yelled "Rapids". The man headed into shore.

When the man landed and climbed out of his canoe Crazy Runner saw that he was a mountain of a man. Crazy Runner was taller than almost everyone he had ever met, but this man was several inches taller than he was with a full long beard and he weighed at least 50 pounds more than him. Crazy Runner figured he was maybe 35 years old.

Crazy Runner said, "A little over a mile ahead there is a canyon with several miles of rapids and no place along the shore to land a boat."

"Thank ya," he said, "I'm beholdin to you. My name is Jim Stone, but people call me Big Jim." They shook hands.

"I am called 'Crazy Runner'."

"Funny, you look white not injun."

"I am white. My parents died of the sickness when I was young and I learned a lot from the Cherokee. They gave me that name and I liked it."

Big Jim said, "What cha doin round here?"

"Just out looking around."

Big Jim laughed with a loud laugh and said, "How long have you been lookin round?"

Crazy Runner thought and said, "What month is it?"

Big Jim said, "I think it be September."

"Well then, I guess a little over five months."

Big Jim gave a big hearty laugh again.

Crazy Runner said, "I have caught several fish, will you share supper with me?"

"Right glad to."

As they ate, Big Jim told him that he was looking for a place for some people to settle that would have good water and good land for planting a crop and no Indian problems. He had seen this river before when he had been coming down the Ohio River but had not been down it before. He had never been in this area of "Kentuck" before.

"How much of 'Kentuck' have you seen?" Big Jim asked.

"Well I have been all the way to the 'Big River'."

"Wow, that there is a powerful amount of 'lookin' round'. You done an awful lot of travelin for bein' so young. You ain't even old enough to grow a beard." He gave another big laugh.

Crazy Runner had heard that Indians did not grow hair on their faces like white men and since Indians were the only people he had been around for several months, except for the Frenchmen, he had not really thought about it.

Big Jim described in a little more detail about the type of land he was looking for these people to settle on.

Crazy Runner told him, "I have seen several places like that west of here, but the Creeks and Shawnees are after each other and it is not good place for white men right now."

"How you know that?"

Crazy Runner told about being captured by the Shawnee, running the gauntlet, and later running into the Creek headed toward the Shawnee village. When he finished, Big Jim said, "You already done a lot of livin' for a young'n."

Crazy Runner added, "I do know a couple of places south of here like that in Cherokee country. If your people are honest and keep to themselves I think the Cherokee might let them settle there."

"Will you show me?"

"Sure, but you will have to walk. I don't know of any rivers leading that way. I just pay attention to where I walk and run."

Big Jim laughed again and said, "You show me the land and then we can figure out how to get the people there."

The next morning they hid Big Jim's canoe and headed off south. When they came to a high hill and Crazy Runner looked to the east, he could see the mountains that looked blue many miles away. He would always remember those mountains because they were the first mountains he had ever seen or been in. Those mountains were like home. He just kept those mountains at about the same distance as he headed south.

CHAPTER 15—TRAVELING

As they traveled, they talked.

Big Jim said, "You know the French are raising a lot of trouble west of the Appalachians in order to keep the English out."

"What are the Appalachians?" Crazy Runner asked.

"Theys those blue like mountains that you keep lookin' at over to the east."

Crazy Runner said, "I guess I don't know the names of things. I just called them the Blue Mountains because in the morning and evening that is what they look like from a distance."

"You're right about that and a lot of people call them the same thing you do."

"You called this land 'Kentuck'."

"Many English people call the land west of Virginia as Virginia. However, the injuns think the mountains and rivers divide the country up. They say the land west of the Appalachians and south of the Ohio River is Kentucky. I am not sure of what it means. I've heard some tribes call in "Bloody Land" because of some great injun wars fought here abouts a long time ago."

Crazy Runner asked, "You said the French were trying to stir up trouble. Why is that?"

"Well there are French up north and down south and a lot of injuns in between. The injuns south of the Ohio are mostly Cherokee, Creek, Chickasaw, and Shawnee. The Ohio River is the easiest way for white men to get from the colonies to west of the Appalachians. It is wide and don't have much in the way of rapids and such. The French want to control both sides of the Ohio River so they can get money from the new English settlers.

The Shawnee is mostly along the river on both sides. Most of the time they put up with the white men traveling on the river and trading with them; but they don't like white men settling in areas that are sacred to them.

The Creeks have been lifelong enemies of the Shawnee and Cherokee. They had a powerful long war that ended about a dozen year ago with the Cherokee and ended up with the Creek movin' further west.

The Chickasaw and Cherokee are mostly friendly towards the white man as long as the white man don't try to get to pushy. They have little frictions with each other, but not many big wars.

Rumor has it that the French want to move settlers into 'Kentuck'. So they is trying to make an agreement with the Creek to push the other tribes and English out of the area so the Frenchies can move in and claim the area and the new settlers will have to buy the land from them."

Crazy Runner said, "I saw some Frenchmen meeting with the Creek a couple of weeks ago west of here."

"What were they doing?"

"I don't know. I ran into three Frenchmen and spent the night in their camp. They said they were trying to set up trading with the Creek. When the Creek showed up they spoke French with them and I didn't understand a word. They talked about thirty minutes and then the Creeks left. The next morning I headed west and the French headed south back to Fort Toulouse."

"Were the Frenchies carrying any trade goods or did the Creeks bring any pelts?"

"No."

"If the Frenchies were really trying to set up trading they would have brought some of their best trade goods to try to convince the Creeks that they would be better off trading with them instead of the English. You probably witnessed the planning for that attack you saw about to happen."

"Later, I saw one of the same Frenchmen with the Creeks that were getting ready to attack the Shawnee village."

They walked in silence for some time with both of them thinking of the consequences of what a war like that would bring about.

Big Jim asked, "You need to be careful around here. Supposedly, when you get to near the southern end of the Appalachians there is a special Cherokee village of much importance to them, sort of a religious thing. It is so important that no white man has ever been there and lived."

"That is Kituhwa," Crazy Runner said, "That is the village I spent some time in. They gave me three tests and I passed them so I was allowed to live among them."

"What were these tests," asked Big Jim.

Crazy Runner answered, "I was told to never reveal the tests. I gave my word so I can't tell you."

"I respect that. What can you tell me about the Cherokee?"

"Well, they believe in balance and honesty. If you take something, then you have to replace it. If you give your word, then you must not go back on it. They will trust a man until that man proves untrustworthy. If the man ever proves untrustworthy then they will kill him.

Let me ask you, why do the English want to move to this side of the Appalachians?"

"Land. There are more and more people coming over here from all over Europe. Every time new people come, they want land to plant crops. Between the Appalachians and the ocean, there is only so much land and the first people here own that. So when new people come then they must move west to find new land. There are many people already moving across the land into the Ohio territory. Those who would like to be by themselves and settle new areas are wanting to move to Kentuck. A group of settlers back at the headwaters of the Ohio are willing to pay good money if I find them a good spot to settle. I will share that money with you if you can help me."

"I don't have much use for money," Crazy Runner said. "Anything I need I trade pelts for it or I make it myself."

"Boy is you sure you is only 17 year old? I knowd full grown men can't do all that."

Chapter 16—Land

After two more days, they reached the first place that Crazy Runner had thought of when Big Jim had described what he was looking for. As they stood on a high rock Crazy Runner pointed out it was a valley about 10 miles long and about two miles wide with a river running through the middle of it. There were several streams running from the hills on both sides down to the river.

There were many deer in the area and a few bears, the rest of the game were small, like rabbits and squirrels. Crazy Runner thought that a lot of the game would probably leave after men started settling in the valley.

Then Crazy Runner pointed out that this was considered Cherokee land, but there were no Cherokee villages in the valley. The closest village was about one day's walk. Big Jim said, "This valley is exactly what them folks is looking for."

They went to the Cherokee village and Crazy Runner explained what Big Jim had told him, that white men wanted to move into the valley and raise crops just like the Cherokee.

The Cherokee agreed, but with the stipulation that the white men must stay inside the hills for any hunting and perhaps trade with the Cherokee.

Big Jim was very happy.

He then wanted to scout around the valley to see if perhaps there was another way into the valley by water that led north to the Ohio so all the people had to do was float from the headwaters of the Ohio to the valley.

Big Jim asked Crazy Runner to travel with him to scout the valley and then back to the headwaters of the Ohio. Crazy Runner readily agreed.

They took off to scout the valley. When Crazy Runner had passed through this valley about four to five months ago, he had just run through the valley along the ridge on the south side. This time they would travel along the north ridge.

When they had gotten almost to the far end of the valley, two days later, they found a river flowing through the hills from the north to the valley river. Big Jim smiled his big smile and said, "Now we will follow this river north and hopefully it will end up at the Ohio and not have any rapids."

Crazy Runner warned, "We must keep a good lookout for Creeks."

They stayed on top of the ridge on the east side of the river and followed it north. Within an hour, they spotted some Creeks coming down the river and hid until they had passed by. There were six braves in two canoes with one canoe staying close to each side of the river. They noticed that the Creek did not travel into the valley they were leaving, but turned their canoes around and headed back north.

Big Jim said, "That is good news."

"Why?" Crazy Runner asked.

"Those Creek are not dressed for war. They are simply a hunting party traveling along the river looking for signs of game coming down to the river on both sides, and then they will go ashore and hunt it. Since they did not want to enter our valley, that means they have some superstition about it and they will probably never go into it.

The bad news is that they probably have a village located somewhere along this river. I guess we will just have to find out."

With three braves paddling each canoe, they were making good time going up river. Big Jim was leading and they were running along the ridge trying to stay in cover, but keep up with the Creek to see where they were going. After about two miles, Big Jim was huffing and puffing, so he stopped. He handed Crazy Runner his tomahawk and said, "Leave me a trail to follow by marking the trees along the way about every 50 feet or so."

Without Big Jim slowing him down Crazy Runner was able to not only keep up with the Creeks, but to get ahead of them. He quickly learned how to balance himself and make a mark on the side of a tree while in full motion.

After another couple of miles, the Creek left the main river and headed up another river going west. Crazy Runner stopped and waited for Big Jim. About 20 minutes later Big Jim caught up to him.

Crazy Runner said, "The Creek headed up that river," while pointing where they had gone.

Big Jim quickly put down his pack and got out a thing that was round and about six inches long. He pulled on both ends and it expanded to about 14 or 15 inches long. Then he looked through it.

"They have a village about three miles upstream."

"How do you know that? What is that thing?" asked Crazy Runner.

As he handed it to Crazy Runner, Big Jim said, "It's called a telescope. Here look through it".

Crazy Runner thought this was marvelous. He could see the village three miles away and it looked as though it were only about ¼ of a mile away. He then took it and looked in different directions. He saw several canoes in the main river heading downstream. He looked without the telescope and the canoes looked like small logs floating on the river.

"This is marvelous. I would like to get one and a tomahawk also."

Big Jim said, "I will get you the best that money can buy when we get to the headwaters of the Ohio."

"Why are those letters scratched in it?"

"I put a 'BJ' on everything of mine, thataways if someone steals it, then I have a way of telling it is mine." He then showed him a small BJ carved on his rifle stock and pistol handle. "When we stop for the night it would be a good thing to do to your things."

Crazy Runner said, "There are many more canoes coming downstream." He pointed to where he had seen them as he handed the telescope back to Big Jim.

Big Jim looked for a minute and then said, "There are a lot of them, but I can't tell what tribe they are."

They continued along the ridge at a slow run for another mile. They got to an opening in the trees and Big Jim took out the telescope and looked again. While still looking he said, "That is a big war party of Shawnee. They must be going to pay the Creek back for their raid."

As they watched, they saw the Shawnee land about ½ mile upstream from the river heading towards the Creek village. They saw the Shawnee carry their canoes into the woods. Because the woods were so thick, they could not see where they went. Since it was starting to get dark, Crazy Runner said, "They are probably doing the same thing that the Creek did. They will camp there in small groups and then start moving just before dawn toward the Creek camp."

"Lets us keep heading north a couple of miles on this side of the river before we make camp for the night," Big Jim said.

CHAPTER 17—FINDING A TRAIL

The next morning they were heading north as the sun was coming up. They had traveled about two miles when they started to hear a waterfall. After another mile, they saw the waterfall and the rapids above it. Crazy Runner used the telescope to look down on the waterfalls and rapids above it and recognized the rocks he had jumped on. It looked like he had been closer to the waterfalls than he had thought.

He gave the telescope to Big Jim and pointed out what had happened to him. Then he said, "Surely all of those Shawnee did not come down those rapids, did they?"

Big Jim was looking around with the telescope without saying anything. After a couple of minutes he handed the telescope to Crazy Runner and said, "You see that little point sticking out into the river there, well look at it through the telescope."

Crazy Runner did and saw a worn trail leading into the woods. "What does the trail mean?"

Big Jim answered, "What injuns does is that they carry their canoes around rapids and waterfalls. That trail over there probably leads to somewhere above the rapids. As you can see, that trail is pretty well worn. What we need ta do is ta find our own trail on this side that the settlers can use. I remember animal tracks heading down toward the river a little ways back. I will go back there and check it out and you go down around here and see if you can find a trail that would be easy enough for women and children. I'll meet you back here in a couple of hours."

They split up. Crazy Runner made his way down. The first 100 feet were easy going and then it got steeper, rockier, and harder to get a good footing. He traveled north along the top of this rocky area until it presently became the wall of the canyon with the rapids below. He climbed up to the ridge top and headed south to meet up with Big Jim.

He saw Big Jim coming towards him, so he stopped and waited. When he got there Big Jim said, "That animal trail should be good for going down, did you find anything?"

Crazy Runner answered, "No, it was too steep."

"This ridge top would be pretty easy going for those folk. Now we have to find a good place to land 'em up river. While I was down there I noticed that there was plenty of tree cover. So all the folks have to do is wait in the trees for nightfall and then float on by the entrance to that river that leads to the Creek village."

Crazy Runner nodded in agreement, as they headed north.

After walking for a couple of hours, they were able to spot the beginning of the trail around the rapids and waterfall on the other side of the river. After another mile, they found a well-worn animal path leading down to the river. This was very easy traveling. They went down to the river and then walked upstream about ½ mile to find markers so they would be able to find the path again.

They found a large boulder on their side with a fallen tree on the other side. The tree was wedged in some rocks so there was little chance it would float away with the spring rains.

They climbed back up to the ridge top and continued heading north. Crazy Runner pointed out the place where he had stolen a canoe.

It took only a few more hours to reach the Ohio River. Again, they marked where on the Ohio River that this river took off. It was just after a big bend in the Ohio River with a large sand bar opposite.

CHAPTER 18—HEADWATERS OF THE OHIO

As they walked up the southern bank of the Ohio Crazy Runner asked, "What is the name of the town at the headwaters of the Ohio?"

"There isn't really a town there. It is where the Allegheny River and the Mechmenawungihilla Rivers form the Ohio River. According to the injuns Allegheny means "fine river" and Mechmenawungihilla means "high banks", but most white people call it the Monongahela. It is easy to get to on land or one of the rivers and from there you can easily travel a long distance to the west away from where most people are settling.

Each time I go back I don't know if the traders I see there will be English or French, but there are always a lot of English there waiting for a guide to the west."

Crazy Runner asked, "How long does it take to get there from here?"

"Walking, I would guess it takes five or six days. If we are lucky there may be a raft going upstream to trade pelts and we can ride with them to help them paddle or pole."

Two days later a raft came along with two men on it. The raft had many pelts tied to it. Big Jim yelled at the raft and one of the men recognized him. They landed the raft and invited Big Jim and Crazy Runner to help them pole their way upstream. Big Jim introduced the two men as Sam Mathews and Ben Jackson.

They were staying close to the shore and using poles. Crazy Runner had not seen anything like this before. Big Jim went and cut two poles. He handed one to Crazy Runner and they got on the raft and pushed away from the shore with the poles. When they got out into the water, then Sam and Ben got on one side and Big Jim and Crazy Runner on the other. The man in front would stick his pole down in the water until it hit bottom and then push along as he walked to the back of the raft. When the first man got to the back, the second man would start from the front and do the same thing. By having two men on each side, it kept a constant forward motion going straight, if the men on the right and left sides were even with each other as they were walking backwards. After Crazy Runner got into the rhythm, they started moving at a good pace. According to Sam, they were moving at lot faster than with just the two of them.

They were able to reach the headwaters of the Ohio late the second day.

For not being a town, there were many people around the area. Many small camps were situated along the rivers, but Big Jim said there were twice as many people camped inland.

As soon as they landed Big Jim and Crazy Runner helped Sam and Ben to carry their pelts to the traders. Big Jim had explained that in the woods, you could trust almost anyone you meet, but around here, there were many crooks who were just too lazy to work for a living. They would just wait for unsuspecting trappers to land, go off and leave their raft. Then they would steal the raft and pelts, take them elsewhere and sell them. Between the four of them, they were able to get all of the pelts in one trip. Crazy Runner had pelts stacked so high in this arms that he could barely see where to walk.

As soon as the pelts were delivered, they said their goodbyes and then Big Jim and Crazy Runner headed inland. They had walked about an hour, during which the sun had gone down, when they came to a camp. During their walk Big Jim explained that the man the group had elected as their leader was a good organizer. He had questioned Big Jim about every facet of the trip and promised that every person would have their duties assigned and understood by the time he got back. Big Jim walked right into the middle of the camp and was warmly welcomed. There were about 40 to 50 men, women, and children in this camp.

Crazy Runner was standing a little behind Big Jim and taking it all in. The man Big Jim was talking to appeared to be the one in charge of the group. After about ten minutes, Big Jim stepped back next to Crazy Runner and introduced Crazy Runner to the man, Hank Jacobs. Big Jim explained to Hank that it was Crazy Runner who showed him this valley. In addition, Crazy Runner had worked it out with the Cherokee to allow them to settle there. Hank shook Crazy Runner's hand and thanked him and then he said, "When can we leave? Winter snows will be starting in a couple of weeks."

Big Jim said, "Day after tomorrow. I want a day and two nights to have some fun first and then we will head out. I need an advance on what you owe me. I promised Crazy Runner that I would buy him a good tomahawk and telescope and I also need a little money for my good time."

Hank gave Big Jim a couple of dollars and said, "That is for your good time. We have men here who are skilled at doing many things and they have made tomahawks and telescopes much better than what you can buy at those tents. I will see he gets a good one of each."

Big Jim said, "Boy, you are still too young to be around some of the places I am going so, I will see you the morning after tomorrow. These nice people will make sure you are fed. We are going to be traveling with them so get to know them and let them get to know you."

Big Jim left and then Crazy Runner and Hank started around to some of the tents and Hank helped him to pick out a good tomahawk and telescope.

Hank asked, "How long will it take to get there?"

Crazy Runner answered, "I am not sure exactly, walking it would take about three to four weeks, but based on what Big Jim has told me about traveling on the river I would say a little over a week. Both rivers flow fast and with a little help we should be able to make it in about eight or nine days. Where are your rafts?"

"We have them built and hidden over there in that brush. What if our stock has problems with the rafts?"

"Well, I guess as long as we are down the Ohio a little ways and can get to the other shore; I could lead some men and the animals there overland. Men and animals should be able to make it, but women and children might have problems."

"That sounds like it will work! I am glad Big Jim found you. You seem very young to be so experienced. Do you mind me asking how that happened?"

Crazy Runner proceeded to tell him about himself. He did a little embellishment about his exploits with the Cherokee and Shawnee.

Chapter 19—The Trip Begins

During the intervening day, Hank had introduced Crazy Runner to all of the people in the group. The night before there had been a big campfire and Crazy Runner explained to everyone there about the valley. He also made sure that they understood the agreement with the Cherokee in that they could not leave the valley to hunt. He finished by telling them, "If you do that the things I have explained to you then the Cherokee will honor the agreement and not cause you any problems. If you raise extra crops, they might even want to trade with you."

As promised, Big Jim showed up early in the morning. Hank had made sure that everyone was already assigned to a raft, including at least one person who was experienced with rafts on each. Hank had made sure that the weight on each raft would be about the same and there were enough people to pole each raft. Crazy Runner was shocked that there were 22 rafts; the smallest one was almost twice as large as Sam and Ben's raft. Eight of them had small corrals on them to hold the horses, mules and cows they had brought with them. Each raft was rectangular so that it would easily fit in some of the narrow areas of the river. Crazy Runner was glad that they had the horses and mules, because some of these rafts were so big that it would be very difficult for men to haul them up the hill to go around the waterfalls.

About two hours after sunrise, the rafts were in the water with everything and everyone loaded. Big Jim was on the first raft and Crazy Runner was on the last raft just to make sure no one got lost. They floated out into the Allegheny River. After about two miles, they reached the Ohio River and started down it.

There was at least one woman on each raft whose responsibility was to make sure the men who were polling were given water and food. Because of this, they did not have to stop for a meal, but could keep going all day.

By the middle of the afternoon, there were already some large gaps between some of the rafts. Big Jim would yell from the front to close up and that message was passed back from raft to raft. The straggling rafts started to close up. It was easy to see that some of them were really struggling, as this type of repetitive and boring work was not what they were used to. Crazy Runner told the men on his raft and the raft ahead of him to take their eyes off the water every now and then and see what kind of game they could see on the shores. This had taken some of the monotony out of it for him and it seemed to work for the men on those rafts.

On the first day, they had traveled further than Crazy Runner had on Sam and Ben's raft going upstream for almost two days. Big Jim had been correct about this being a faster and easier method of travel for large groups.

That night some of the men were talking and wondering

whether they would be able to get homes built before the winter snows came. Crazy Runner asked, "What is winter snow?"

One of the men replied, "You mean you have never seen snow?"

Crazy Runner said, "I don't know, what does it look like?"

The men laughed, then another said, "It is when it gets real cold and then white snowflakes fall from sky. They cover the ground and trees and everything turns white until it warms up to melt the snow."

"I would like to see that. I have seen some white things falling from the sky, but I have never seen them turn the trees and ground white." Crazy Runner said.

"You mean there is no snow in this valley we're headin' to?" a man asked.

"No, it gets cold enough to where you must wear more clothes but I have never seen anything white fall from the sky around there."

The men started yelling and jumping around. Crazy Runner could not understand why they were so happy. Big Jim came over and asked what all the noise was about. One of the men told him, "Crazy Runner said that it does not snow in this valley where we're headin'. He says he had never seen snow accumulate on the ground."

Big Jim answered, "It does not snow every winter in that territory, but there are snow storms around that part of the country every few years."

"How cold does it get?" he was asked.

"It gets cold, but not usually cold enough to freeze water."

Crazy Runner had a little trouble understanding exactly what all of the excitement was about since the Carolina weather was all he had experienced, except for his traveling this year.

The third day they made it to the mouth of the river leading to the valley.

On the fifth day, they made it to where they had to land to go around the waterfalls. Hank already had informed everyone what his or her duties were. As soon as the rafts landed all of the women got as much as they could carry and Big Jim had Crazy Runner lead them up to the ridge top. They found a large opening and placed things on the ground. Some of the women went back down to help carry more things up while the rest of the women and children made camp for that night.

Crazy Runner scouted down the mountain ridge to about a mile past the trail they were going to take down to the river. He stopped several times to check out the entire area with his new telescope. By the time Crazy Runner had gotten back to the where they were bringing the rafts up they already had the six largest rafts up to the ridge top. Shortly after dark, the last of the rafts was up to the ridge top. Several of the men cut down some brush and used it to cover the trail up to the ridge top.

When they got to the camp Big Jim reminded everyone how important it was to remain quiet and not start any fires, when a woman came up and handed him a piece of hot meat. He started to get mad when she said, we found a small cave on the side of this hill away from the river and lit a cook fire in it so the fire cannot be seen and no one will see the smoke at night. Big Jim smiled and said, "Thanks."

The next day everyone helped move everything to the top of the trail leading down to the river that was past the rapids and waterfall. They slowly moved the rafts down to areas about 15 to 20 feet above the river, but still hidden behind heavy brush. All of this was completed about two hours before sunset.

Everyone rested until about two hours after sunset, the work progressed very methodically and quietly to get the rafts loaded

CRAZY RUNNER - TRAILBLAZER - 1750

and down to the water. About four hours before sunrise, they took off. Big Jim had warned everyone that they must stay very close and very quiet until about noon.

At the end of the eighth day, they were within sight of the canyon that held their valley on the other side. Big Jim did not want to take any chances so they kept going well into the night until they were actually inside their valley. At that point, there was a lot of whooping and hollering coming from each raft. They camped along the shore and could have campfires.

The next morning they continued floating down the river until it intersected with the river that ran the length of the valley. Then they landed the rafts on the east shore and had a large meeting. In that meeting Crazy Runner spoke to them, "Everything within these hills is yours to use. The Cherokee have given you this right. This valley is in Cherokee territory. As long as you do not go over these mountains to hunt and are not hostile to any Cherokee you see, then you may remain here. If you travel back up that river, you have to look out for the Creeks who are friends of the French and enemies of the Cherokee. They will probably attack you, but they should not come into this valley. The river running the length of the valley runs out of the valley to the west, but that also is Creek territory."

Hank then took over the meeting and said they would make a camp right here. This would be their settlement. Then the men would begin scouting the valleys and picking out their places to build their homes. They would begin by immediately building one large building at this location to have future meetings and celebrations. He explained they would call the big building their Settlement House and could use it for everyone to live in should this prove to be one of the bad winters.

Crazy Runner said to Big Jim, "I like Hank! He has everything well planned out. He is a good leader."

"That is the only reason I agreed to find them some land. I have had other people ask me, but because of his ability to plan things and the way the others listened to him, I knew this was a group that would make it. What are you going to do now Crazy Runner?"

"I don't know. I have learned a lot from you and would like to travel with you for a while, if that is alright with you?"

Big Jim answered, "I would like that very much. We will leave in several days after we make sure that everything is ok with these folks. I thought you and I might do some hunting for them while they are building their large house. After we are sure they have plenty of food and are on the way to making a home here, then we can leave."

Chapter 20—Heading North

With all of the men working together, it took only two days for them to clear an area for the Settlement House they were planning. After that was accomplished Hank had divided the men into four groups: one group to gather rocks for the foundation and chimney, one group to cut trees and haul them to the area where the Settlement House was to be built, one group to clean the logs so they could be used for building or flooring planks, and the last group to start on the foundation and do the actual building.

Big Jim and Crazy Runner had killed two bears and many deer for the settlers. Big Jim had asked Crazy Runner if he would like to see snow and Crazy Runner immediately had said "yes". The hides of the two bear were prepared to be made into winter coats for Big Jim and Crazy Runner.

After a week, the Settlement House was finished and everyone had claimed a small portion inside as their place to stay until their own cabin was built. The men started around the valley looking for places to settle and build their own places.

The next week was when Big Jim and Crazy Runner decided to head north.

First, they headed to the Cherokee village just over the mountains to the east. Crazy Runner informed the Cherokee that the settlers were there and beginning to make their homes.

A Cherokee Chief asked Crazy Runner, "What is the purpose of the very big house they have built. Is it some type of fort?"

Crazy Runner was not surprised that they already knew of the Settlement House. He explained, "They have a very smart chief. He had them build the Settlement House first so everyone would have a place to go for shelter in case of bad weather. After their own homes are built, they will use the Settlement House for tribal meetings. It will also be used as a fort against the Creek, but the Cherokee will always be welcome."

The Chief responded, "Yes, he is a smart chief. We will have to meet with him when the warm weather returns."

Big Jim and Crazy Runner spent the night in the Cherokee village and the next morning headed north. They decided the traveling would be easiest along the highest ridges. They headed immediately towards the top of the Appalachians.

When they got there, they headed north along the ridge tops. Whenever they got to a place where they could see a distance, they marveled at the beauty of the trees changing colors. The further north they got the trees were differing colors with more reds and oranges.

At one point, there was a large gap in the Appalachian Mountains where the mountains dropped considerably in height. The low area was several miles wide. As they came to a river Big Jim said, "Several months ago I was here and came upon a man named Dr. Thomas Walker. He named this river the Cumberland after some famous Englishman who won some big battle a few years ago. On the east side of this gap in the mountains, you have Virginia and it is only a short distance to the Carolinas and on the west side is Kentucky. The Indians have been using this gap for a very long time as an easy way to get through the mountains."

In the second week, it was getting very cold at night. They would camp on the opposite side of the ridge from the wind to help with the cold. Near the end of the second week, they were hit with an ice storm, which had freezing rain and hail dropping on them. They were lucky in that they found a small cave that was large enough for the two of them and a fire. They took turns going out into the weather getting wood for the fire. The storm lasted two days.

They were both getting anxious to be moving. Neither of them liked being confined in a small space for very long. When the storm finally broke and the sun came out, they decided to continue their journey. Crazy Runner was leading and it was not long before he slipped on the ice and went sliding about ten feet downhill until he landed against a tree.

Big Jim was just standing there laughing. Then he said, "I could have told you how slippery ice is, but you might have forgotten. After that spill you will never forget." Then they both laughed.

Big Jim said, "Get up slowly. There are some tricks to staying on your feet on ice. The best is to always take small steps and walk flat-footed. Never walk on rocks like you just did, always try to walk where there is grass. If you are heavy enough to break through the ice on the grass then that will help you stay on your feet.

Sometimes the ice on ponds or lakes or rivers becomes so thick that you can walk on it"

"You can't walk on water."

"No, but you can walk on ice if the ice is thick enough. That is what you have to be careful of. If the ice is not thick enough and you go through the ice, you will get so wet that you will freeze to death unless you can get a fire built right away. There are many other lessons you need to learn about the winter weather, but those can wait."

They slowly headed north.

Chapter 21—Snow

    They had traveled for about an hour when the sun finally came out from behind the clouds. Crazy Runner was amazed at the beauty of the sun hitting the trees and bushes covered with ice. He just stopped and looked all around for about fifteen minutes. Big Jim said nothing and just watched him and the amazement in his eyes and expression. Big Jim had seen this scene many times before and had forgotten how wonderful it looked the first time he had seen it. That made him even more anxious for them to get further north and see snow.
    Because of the ice, they had traveled as far in one hour as they usually did in ten minutes. As they continued traveling north, they got out of the ice by noon, which made the traveling much easier. Late that afternoon, they topped a ridge and lying in front of them was an entire valley covered in snow with the sun glistening on it. Crazy Runner sat down on a rock and just looked. This morning he had thought the ice looked beautiful, but this was the most wonderful thing he had ever seen. He sat

there motionless for about an hour taking it all in. Big Jim would look at the snow, then look at him and back again.

They found a nestling of trees and bushes that provided a good windbreak and proceeded to make camp. Crazy Runner got some wood and started to make a fire in under the trees. Big Jim immediately stopped him and said, "This is one lesson I am going to tell you because I am cold and want a warm fire. The heat from the fire will go up. What do you see directly above where you have placed the wood?"

"Tree limbs with snow on them."

"When the heat reaches that snow then the snow will fall and put the fire out and you will have to start all over again. You need to have the fire in a place that has no snow above it."

The way Big Jim had explained it made sense. Crazy Runner moved the wood about four feet to one side and got the fire started. They had a warm meal and watched the moon making the snow sparkle.

Crazy Runner said, "While this is very pretty, it can also be very dangerous."

"That is correct," Big Jim answered. "If we go further north then you will really have problems. When the wind blows the snow, sometimes the snow can cover deep holes. If you go through the snow you may break a leg and be stuck in the hole. To be safe, tomorrow, before we start, we will each cut a long branches, like when we were poling the raft. As we walk, we will poke holes in the snow to find where the ground is and if it is strong enough to walk on. You especially want to do this whenever you are walking across a frozen stream, river, or lake. The snow here is not deep enough for us to really worry about, but it will give you good practice."

The next day they came to a river. They could hear the water under the snow, but they could not see the water. Big Jim explained, "This is what I was warning you about." They slowed down and carefully prodded the ground in front of them with their tree limbs. It did not take long before they found where the edge of the river was and that the ice was very thin. With little effort, the limbs broke through the ice into the water.

They broke open a hole in the ice, got a drink and noticed which direction the water was flowing. They then headed upstream because rivers were usually at their narrowest upstream.

Crazy Runner had noticed the tracks of several animals in the snow. He was amazed at how easy it was to tell from a distance what type of animal was leaving the tracks. The problem was that unless he knew when the snow fell and how much snow fell at that time then he could not tell whether this animal had left these tracks one hour ago or one week ago.

Crazy Runner knew he was getting an excellent education from Big Jim. The overseer's wife had taught him to read and do his numbers, but Big Jim was teaching him about life.

While in the snow, Big Jim said it would make it easier to teach him about backtracking. "Just like you can track animals, Indians on the war path can track you. You already know that if you travel on rocks it is very difficult to follow the trail."

"Unless you can find rocks which have been moved by having the weight of something on top of them," Crazy Runner added.

"That is correct. Sometimes it is easier to lead the ones tracking you on a false trail. To do this you first need to find somewhere to leave the trail that will not be easy to follow. Then you need to continue on the trail for some time until you come to some place else to leave the trail in a different direction. Once you have found the second place you back up carefully stepping in your previous tracks until you get to the first place, then you leave the trail. If you have done a good job of carefully stepping in your own tracks, those following will follow the second trail and not the first. It is easiest to practice this in snow. So I now want you to stop and retrace your steps back to that log we stepped over about twenty feet back."

Crazy Runner did this. He quickly found that he had to keep a constant motion or he would leave too deep a track and that would let the follower know he had backtracked.

Then Big Jim told him, "You have to be more careful in snow or when the ground is wet, because your feet have to be in exactly the same places with no mistake at all. On dry ground, it is a little easier to backtrack.

You have already learned about tracking large animals not only by their marks on the ground, but also by their marks on the bushes and trees they pass. If you are being tracked you have to be careful to not leave any type of trail.

You are a good person, so I don't believe any injuns who know who you are will be tracking you. The ones you have to look for are those injuns on the warpath. They will be after anyone."

Crazy Runner said, "Except for that one time with the Creek, I have not seen Indians on the war path. What causes Indians to go to war?"

"It can be anything. Most Indians are very proud and very protective of what they believe is theirs. White men buy land and consider it theirs. Indians consider themselves as protectors of the land for their god. Food is what is most important, they do not want anyone else hunting in areas that they hunt because they feel that will shorten the food supply for their families."

"That makes sense," Crazy Runner replied.

"Just like white men have feuds that last for generations, so do injuns. I once knew two white families that had been feuding since before they came to this country and they continued to feud when they got here. The thing that no one in either family could tell me was how the feud got started and some injun feuds are the same way."

CHAPTER 22—MASSACRE

They traveled along the tops of the Appalachians for two more days. At the top of one peak, they could see many towns and farms to the east with their telescopes. They looked to the west and could see only one small village and a few farms.

Suddenly they noticed smoke coming from the west. They turned their telescopes in that direction and saw a fire. Some type of building was on fire. It was several miles off, but they headed in that direction, because there might be someone there who needed help.

Crazy Runner knew that he could reach the farm in about one hour, but Big Jim could not run that fast. Big Jim told him to go ahead and blaze a trail as he went, but be very careful because it was possible the fire had been set by a war party.

Crazy Runner took off with his tomahawk in his hand making sure to leave a mark on a tree about every 10 to 12 steps. When he had gotten to within eyesight of the fire, he saw it was a cabin on fire. He also saw the tracks of many Indians. He immediately stopped running and carefully looked around. He kneeled down

CRAZY RUNNER - TRAILBLAZER - 1750

and was motionless for about five minutes, while looking in all directions. He was not able to hear or see anything, so he slowly and carefully walked up to the cabin.

As he reached the cabin, he saw the bodies of eight persons lying on the ground. Three of them were Indians. One was a large man about 40. One was a woman close to 40. Then there were two boys one about Crazy Runners age and one about two or three years younger. The last was a little girl about four or five. All of them had some of the top of their head cut off. It was a horrifying sight to see.

Crazy Runner had completed a search of the burned cabin and around the edge of the clearing by the time Big Jim arrived. Big Jim took one look and said, "This is no 'Mourning War', there is a reason for this."

"What is a 'Mourning War'?"

"The dead Indians are Seneca, one of the Iroquois tribes. Whenever they lose people in battle, they go to war and capture slaves to take the place of those who have died.

This is different, the French and English started paying money to the Indians for the scalps of white settlers who were in areas that they did not want them in. When part of the top of the head is gone like that they have taken that scalp to have someone pay them for it."

"That is horrible."

"Yes, it is. That is the price of bringing civilization to these so-called heathens. Personally, I think the injuns were much better off before white man's civilization arrived," Big Jim said.

"Where are the Iroquois?"

"The Iroquois is a name given to six tribes who joined together in a peaceful way; that is until the white men arrived. The six tribes are the Seneca, Mohawks, Oneida, Cayuga, Tuscarora and Onandaga. They usually stay north of the Ohio

River, except on raids. The Seneca have their lands closest to here. Lately the Tuscarora and Oneida have been friendly with the English, but the Seneca and the other Iroquois Nations have been friendly with the French.

It is unusual to see them this far south. Many years ago there were some big wars and the Cherokee, Creek, and Shawnee pushed most of the Iroquois tribes north of the Ohio River."

It took them the rest of the day to bury the five whites individually. They dug one large grave and put all three Indians in it.

When they finished with the burials, they found a place with good wind cover and made camp for the night.

The next day they decided to track the Seneca for a day or two just to see if there were any more whites who needed to be buried.

Chapter 23—A Bigger Massacre

The next day Crazy Runner and Big Jim found two more settler families that had been murdered and scalped by the Seneca. It took most of the day to bury the nine people.

The second day they began to get worried. The Seneca were not trying to cover their tracks and they found that they had met with a much larger group of Indians and all were now headed west. Big Jim figured out exactly where they were headed and told Crazy Runner, "About two days walk from here is a new fort, it looks like they are headed there to wipe out that fort and get a lot more scalps."

"We are behind them by a couple of hours, how can we get ahead of them and let the settlers know?"

Big Jim said, "I can't, but you can because you can run at a high speed for a much longer period of time than me. Northwest of here a little ways is a stream. If you follow it upstream to that little mountain over there and follow that ridge west, you will see the fort from the ridge. It will take a lot of running; but you should get there by early morning and it will take them until tomorrow night at the earliest to get there. While injuns can run also, they don't like to when they are in large groups because it is too noisy and they can't sneak up on anyone. I will follow them and make sure that is where they are headed. If they change directions I will come to the fort and let you know."

"I will see you there," Crazy Runner said as he took off heading northwest through the thick brush running full speed.

It only took about two hours of running at full speed for Crazy Runner to get to the top of the mountain and head west. He never stopped, but he did slow down to walk occasionally to get his full wind back. Just before dark, he spotted the Seneca. He stopped, got out his telescope and looked at them. They had made camp in a large open area. There were about 100 Seneca and he saw two men in military uniforms.

Crazy Runner slowed his run to a trot while he ate some berries. He continued running though the night slowing to a trot whenever clouds blocked the moon and made it difficult to see.

About an hour before dawn, he saw the fort and headed down from the hills at full speed. He reached the fort just before dawn. There was a guard at the gate and as he was running up Crazy Runner yelled, "Let me in, there's a war party coming."

As the gates opened, a bell started ringing. It did not take long for a crowd to gather and more were running in from the surrounding area. Crazy Runner said, "Three families about two days east of here were murdered and scalped by the Seneca. There is a large war party headed in this direction. I couldn't tell much from the distance but it looked to be about 100 Indians and I saw two men in military uniforms with them. It will be late today or early tomorrow before they are here."

"Must be the French." one man said.

Another man started pointing to specific men to go in different directions to get the settlers in the area outside the fort.

One of the women started yelling out things for the women and children to do. Crazy Runner noticed that everyone was remaining calm and no one was panicking.

Crazy Runner said to a man standing next to him, "You people been through this type of thing before?"

"Yep," as he spit some tobacco juice, "We been here a little over a year and this be the fourth injun attack. It is unusual for them to attack in cold weather like this. Mighty lucky for us you seen them or else we would not have been ready for them."

Crazy Runner thought that might be the reason why the Indians had chosen this time to attack; they figured the settlers would not be alert.

The women were working gathering water and making sandwiches for the men. They also set up in the store to be ready to reload rifles and pistols. The men were helping others to get to the fort and setting up positions around the walls of the fort. It looked like each man already had his assigned position and each man was setting up things the way he liked them at his place.

By noon every man, woman, and child within a couple of miles in every direction was inside the fort. As soon as each man had his place around the wall set up a guard schedule was established. Starting in the early afternoon the men started taking naps in any comfortable warm place they could find.

Crazy Runner asked one man, "The Seneca are about to attack. Why are the men taking naps?"

The man answered, "The Seneca are not that superstitious about attacking at night like the Shawnee and Creek. By getting some rest now, they will be more alert whenever the attack does come. We sent two men out in slightly different directions to give us advanced warning when they see them."

"What do you want me to do?" asked Crazy Runner.

"Sit and be patient. When the attack comes, you just watch around the wall and take the place of someone who has been killed or wounded."

That seemed to make sense, but Crazy Runner felt like he should do something. He helped some of the women fetch water. He helped filling up powder horns. Then he decided that perhaps he should get some rest also. He found a place and lay down.

He did not have time to get to sleep before both of the lookouts came running back. It was now late afternoon. Both men said they each saw the Indians and they were definitely painted for war. They felt the Indians were about one hour away. Crazy Runner went up to the wall and used his telescope to look to the east. A little over 30 minutes later, he was able to see the Indians approaching. Two other men with telescopes had spotted them at the same time.

Crazy Runner then saw small bands of Seneca taking off in different directions. About an hour later, everyone in the fort could see the smoke from the burning homes. Some of the children became frightened and started crying and their mothers were trying their best to calm them.

Shortly before dark, two men in military uniforms marched up to the fort carrying a white flag. Crazy Runner took a bead on one of the men and the man next to him said, "Don't shoot. That there flag means he wants to talk, peaceable like."

The front gate was opened slightly and the two men marched in. The gate closed after them. The two men marched to almost the center of the fort and stopped. One of them said, "Who is in charge here?" in English with a heavy French accent.

A man stepped forward and said, "My name is Hackett. Speak your piece."

"Mr. Hackett, all of your homes have been burned. You no

longer have any reason to stay here. If you leave this fort at dawn then none of you will be harmed. You may take all of your belongings with you. If you refuse to leave you will all be killed."

There was silence and the two Frenchmen turned to leave only to find Crazy Runner blocking their retreat with his knife in his right hand and tomahawk in his left. Crazy Runner said to the one who had been talking, "How much do you pay the Seneca for white scalps?"

The two Frenchmen looked at each other and said nothing.

"Mister, I asked you a question. If I don't get an answer real fast I am going to scalp both of you and throw those scalps over the wall," Crazy Runner said.

"But we came here under a flag of truce. Civilized men honor the flag of truce."

Hackett said, "That's right. We will honor his flag of truce."

"Do civilized men also pay for scalps? I am going to give you to the count of three to tell me how much you pay or I am going to give them your scalps. One...Two..."

"Alright. We pay them one Franc each."

"What is your rank?"

"I am a Major."

"What is his rank?"

"He is a Lieutenant."

"The way I have it figured you two have no honor. You are trying to lure these people out of their nice safe fort in order for the Seneca to catch them in the open. That way the Seneca can get a lot of money from you for these people's scalps and they don't have to work all that hard for it. That should make you even more popular to them.

Lieutenant, you are going to go out there and tell the Seneca to go back home by tomorrow morning or I am going to scalp the Major."

The Major said, "But that isn't civilized."

"And paying a dollar for each person killed is civilized! Now someone open up the gate and let the Lieutenant out."

The Lieutenant did not move.

Crazy Runner said, "Lieutenant would you prefer me to scalp both of you or just the Major."

At that, the Lieutenant moved rather quickly toward the gate as the folks started laughing. Crazy Runner yelled after him, "Oh Lieutenant, Don't forget to come back to get your Major after the Seneca have gone." The people laughed some more.

Mr. Hackett had some men tie up the Major and put him out of the way. Then he said to Crazy Runner, "How do you know that the Lieutenant won't come back and tell us the Seneca are gone and then we let them go and still get massacred?"

"I thought of that. I have a friend out there who has been trailing the Seneca. As soon as they are gone, he will come and tell us. All we have to do is patiently wait." Patience was a virtue that Crazy Runner usually did not have, unless he was hunting game for a meal.

The Lieutenant came back shortly after the sun came up in the morning and said, "The Seneca are leaving. I had them wait until this morning so you could see them leaving."

Crazy Runner said to Mr. Hackett, "I don't really trust anyone who would pay money for scalps, do you?"

"Nope, I think we better tie him up also until your friend arrives."

"What friend?" the Lieutenant asked.

Crazy Runner said, "I have a friend out there and he is watching your Seneca. When he is sure that they are gone then he will come and let us know. We will wait one day and then let both of you go. If they are not gone, then I will scalp you both. Does that sound alright to you, Mr. Hackett?"

"That sounds fine to me."

The Lieutenant started looking worried. Crazy Runner said to him, "Did you think that we would just let you walk out of here as soon as we saw some of them heading off?" The Lieutenant did not answer.

"Lieutenant, that look tells me that the Seneca were supposed to go just a little ways and then sneak back tonight."

"How did you know?" said the Lieutenant.

"I didn't know for sure until now. Well it looks like the first scalps they are going to get are going to be the scalps of you and the Major." Crazy Runner started to pull out his knife.

The Lieutenant said, "Quickly, untie me and let me get to the top of the wall to signal them so they will really leave."

Hackett immediately untied him. He ran to the ladder and quickly went up to the wall and started waving his hat. After a couple of minutes, an Indian came out from behind a tree. The Lieutenant motioned for him to come up to the fort.

As the Lieutenant climbed down the ladder, he told Crazy Runner that he must tell the Indian to tell the Chief to really leave. Crazy Runner yelled to the men on the wall, "If he tries to run, shoot them both".

The Lieutenant went out the gates and met the Indian about fifteen feet away. They argued loudly for a while and then the Indian left and the Lieutenant came back inside the fort. He told Crazy Runner, "They are leaving for good."

"What was the arguing about?"

"They wanted more goods to replace the money they were going to get from your scalps and I told them they would get it."

Hackett told the Major and Lieutenant, "We might have agreed to move if you had offered us a lot of goods and money."

It was a peaceful night.

The next morning, the Major and Lieutenant wanted to leave. Crazy Runner said, "Not until my friend shows up and lets me know that the Seneca have really left."

The day was very peaceful and relaxing. In fact, the people had even decided to throw a shindig that night. Just before dark, Big Jim showed up at the gate and yelled, "You got a fella named Crazy Runner in there".

They opened the gates and let him in. Most of the people greeted Big Jim with familiar yells and slaps on the back. It was Big Jim who had led them to this area.

Hackett explained to Big Jim about everything that Crazy Runner had done.

Big Jim said, "It looks like you is full growed now. You handled that situation well. What made you think about that plan?"

"You did in telling me about why the Indians take scalps. It just seemed natural that if they paid them for the scalps of those farmers, the injuns would want the same amount of money for the ones in the fort."

Big Jim said, "Well you were right. They headed off yesterday morning only to hide behind hills and in the brush. Then after the one met with that Frenchie they really did leave. I followed them until they started crossing the Ohio River, then I hightailed it back here."

The settlers had a big party that night with a lot of music and food and drink. Big Jim really liked the drink part. Crazy Runner tried some, but it burned his throat as it was going down and he did not like that.

The next morning they freed the Major and Lieutenant. Just before they were walking out the gates Big Jim walked up to them and said, "Major, you know if you did not sleep on your back you probably wouldn't snore so loud. The other night when you were in the clearing east of here, you kept the Lieutenant awake much of the night. I know because I walked right into that camp and no one knew I was there.

The next time I hear of you Frenchies paying for scalps I know about twenty men who can sneak around every bit as good as I can, and we will make it our duty to scalp every Frenchie we can find. We will start with you.

Do you understand me?"

"Oui" and they left the fort.

After they were gone, Crazy Runner asked, "Do you think that speech will actually do any good?"

"Not really, but I sure got his attention didn't I?" They both laughed.

CHAPTER 24—SAVING A WHITE MAN

Two days later Big Jim was over his hangover and they headed south. As they walked along Big Jim was still congratulating Crazy Runner for his strategy back at the camp. Crazy Runner answered that it was what he thought the Cherokee would have done.

"Why are we heading south?"

Big Jim answered, "My old bones are sick and tired of the cold. Plus there is another settlement about a week's walk south of here that I want to check on. I led those people to that place. I feel responsible when I lead people somewheres I think is safe, and they get killed."

"But they knew the risks when they came west with you, didn't they?"

"Sure they did. When I am traveling with the people, I get to know them pretty good and that makes me feel responsible for them.

You don't know this but where these folks come from is a lot of countries which together is called Europe. Others already

CRAZY RUNNER - TRAILBLAZER - 1750

own all of the land, so it is difficult to buy your own land. The rich control everything. They tell you what to do, where you can work, even whether or not you can worship the almighty.

Coming out to this country is their first time to be really free. It is their first time to be able to settle on a piece of land that is theirs. What happens to them is usually in their hands and limited only by how hard they are willing to work. Just by agreeing to come out here, you already know they are willing to work hard and have a lot of grit.

All of them came from similar backgrounds so they want to help each other to be successful. That is what this new land is all about."

They walked in silence for some time so Crazy Runner could let all of that sink in.

Two days later, they were on a narrow animal trail and Crazy Runner was walking behind Big Jim. Suddenly, Big Jim stopped and listened. He quickly turned and motioned for them to go back. About fifty feet back there was a dead tree lying near the trail. Crazy Runner jumped on top of the tree, ran down the top of it and jumped into a large bush with Big Jim right behind him.

They sat there in silence for about ten minutes when they could hear the sounds of running feet and some yelling. A white man came running down the trail at full speed and they could hear Indians behind him.

Crazy Runner started to say something to the white man, but Big Jim put his hand over his mouth and they sat there silent. A few minutes later five Shawnee braves came up the trail whooping and hollering. Crazy Runner saw Big Jim get his tomahawk out and ready and Crazy Runner readied his bow and arrow. As soon as the first four braves had passed, Big Jim stood up and threw his tomahawk at the last brave; it caught him in the side of his head. Crazy Runner understood and immediately threw his tomahawk, it went in the back of the fourth Indian. While his tomahawk was still in flight, Crazy Runner had already jumped up on the fallen tree and shot an arrow into the third Indian. The two Indians in front were concentrating so much on the man they were chasing that they did not realize what was happening behind them.

Big Jim had taken a bead with his rifle on the first Indian and fired just as the third Indian was falling to the ground. The second Indian tripped over the first Indian and stumbled. Big Jim picked up Crazy Runner's rifle and shot the second Indian as he was getting to his feet.

Big Jim told Crazy Runner to load the rifles while he made sure each of the Indians was dead. He got their tomahawks and dragged the dead Indians off the trail just in case there were any more Indians coming up the trail.

When Big Jim was just finishing dragging the last body off the trail, the white man came back. Big Jim motioned for him to be quiet and lead him to where Crazy Runner was.

When they were all concealed Big Jim whispered to the man, "What happened?"

At the same time Crazy Runner said, "This is the Frenchie who was with the Creeks when they raided the Shawnee."

The Frenchman studied Crazy Runner, then said, "The young trapper who likes to run!", and started to give him a hug. Crazy Runner backed away.

"So the Shawnee caught up to you while you were with the Creeks?" Big Jim asked.

"Oui."

"Did you get the Creek to attack the fort about two days south of here?" Big Jim asked. The Frenchman did not answer.

Big Jim immediately pushed the man to the ground and put his knife to his throat while he yelled, "I asked you a question!"

"Oui," the Frenchman said.
"Were they wiped out?"
"Oui."

Big Jim was silent for a moment and then started to slowly get up. His knife flashed in the sunlight as he swiftly stabbed the Frenchman in the stomach and twisted it as he was pulling it out.

The Frenchman screamed in agony as Big Jim got up, grabbed his gear and headed off to the south. Crazy Runner got up and followed Big Jim leaving the Frenchman screaming behind them.

"Why did you do that?" Crazy Runner asked.

Big Jim softly said, "With a wound like that it will take him most of a day to die. In my mind people who pay others to kill deserve to die themselves as painfully as possible. It will serve as a message to others."

Everything had happened so fast, they had walked for some time before Crazy Runner realized he had actually killed his first two humans. He had killed animals before for food, but never for pleasure. However, the more he thought about the white settlers he had buried, the less he regretted it; however, it was not the Shawnees who had killed and scalped the settlers and he really did not know what was happening and just had to follow Big Jim's lead.

Chapter 25—Survivors

After a day and a half, they came across an area where the Shawnee and Creek had battled. There was a lot of blood on the ground. Both tribes had carried off their wounded and dead to be buried according to their custom. The Creeks had headed southeast and the Shawnee had headed northwest.

It took them another day to reach the fort. It had been burned to the ground. In several places, it was still smoldering. Most of the bodies of the dead had been burned beyond recognition. Big Jim had Crazy Runner run in a large circle around the fort searching for any person who might still be alive at outlying farms, while he carefully searched the fort.

Crazy Runner found six farms as he circled around the fort about one mile out. Four of the farms were deserted; evidently, these settlers had gone to the fort. The other two farms each had the two adults and two children, all dead and scalped. Crazy Runner figured it was going to take them several days to bury all of these people.

CRAZY RUNNER - TRAILBLAZER - 1750

It was well after dark when Crazy Runner got back to the fort. He did not see Big Jim anywhere. He got behind some cover and let out the bird whistle Big Jim had taught him as a signal. Big Jim stepped out of the trees at the edge of the clearing and motioned for Crazy Runner to come there.

When Crazy Runner got there, he was amazed to find a woman and five children, two boys and three girls all between four and ten years old. Big Jim said, "I told these folks to build a place to hide valuables and children during attacks. When I found it, they were in it. The woman would sneak out to get food and water for the children and then would go back in. As soon as it was dark and the children couldn't really see everything that had happened I led them all here."

"What are we going to do with them?" Crazy Runner asked.

Big Jim said, "While I was waiting for you I gave that a lot of thought. The way I see it, we need to do two things: get these people to safety and warn Hank Jacobs settlement that the Creeks are on the warpath. I think it best if we split up. I will take these folks back to Hackett's Fort and tell him and you go warn Hank Jacobs settlement, which I figure is about seven or eight days walk from here, but you could probably make it in three days if you don't run into any Creek."

"That sounds like a good plan. I will leave at dawn."

The next morning Crazy Runner and Big Jim were up before the woman and children were. Big Jim said, "It took you and I almost four days to get here, but the youngsters will tire easily and it will probably take us about six days to get there.

You need to be careful because you are going to be heading right through the middle of Creek territory. We already know they are getting paid for white scalps and they are really mad at getting run off by the Shawnee, so be very careful."

"I will." They shook hands and Crazy Runner started off, not sure if he would ever see Big Jim again.

Chapter 26—Dangerous Journey

Crazy Runner figured that he could run fast for the first day until he saw some sign of the retreating Creek. He knew they had to be two days ahead of him. The snow had been beautiful, but it was nice to be in an area without snow. It made the running much easier. It was cold, but not as cold as it had been when he had been around the ice and snow. The running kept him good and warm.

Most of this area was low hills and solid with trees and shrubbery. He was hoping for a high ridge he could travel along, to avoid the valleys and have a better vantage point of the surrounding area.

He had run full out for about six hours, it was well into the afternoon. He came to a stream and decided to rest for a few minutes and get a drink. As he lay there by the stream, he heard something in the brush on the other side of the stream and quickly scampered into some brush on his side. Four Creek came out of the brush and got a drink. Crazy Runner thought that if had kept running across that stream he would have run straight into them.

The Creek stayed there for a while and then they went back the way they had come. Crazy Runner quietly went downstream on this side of the stream staying well back from the stream and out of view. He did not dare run for a while. In fact, he could not even walk fast, because he could not make any noise.

After about an hour, Crazy Runner crossed the stream and continued southeast. He was walking a little faster now, but still concentrating on being quiet. He was making sure that he stayed off human trails and only on animal trails. He was also careful to leave as few signs as possible.

The animal trail he was on was heading up a hill and that was good. Hopefully, he could find a concealed place where he had a good view of the surrounding area. He got near the top of the hill when he heard talking.

He quickly got off the trail and hid in some brush. The talking was Indian and coming from in front of him. The way it sounded, they were not moving. He was glad they were talking or he would have run right into them. He backtracked about 100 yards and headed through the brush heading east. When he had gone about a mile, he turned south and headed back up toward the ridge.

When he got to the top of the ridge he used his telescope to look back along the ridge and saw a Creek burial ground. The Creeks he had heard talking were either burying someone or protectors of the burial ground.

To the east, just below the ridge, he saw a Creek village. He saw another smaller camp to the south and one to the north. Off to the southeast many miles he could see the mountains that contained Hank Jacobs valley.

Crazy Runner knew that there would be many Indians

traveling from the village to one of the smaller camps. In a few small clearings, he was able to see a few Indians doing just that.

It was now late in the afternoon. What he would do is to go slowly down this hill heading between the village to the east and the camp to the south. He would wait until well after dark and then continue between the two. He found some thick brush and rested until about two hours after full dark. He was glad that it was a cloudy night.

He walked bent over most of the time making sure that his head was at the level of the bushes around him and not above them. He could see the fire from the camp, but the hill blocked his view of the village. The campfires from the village helped keep him in the direction he needed to go.

After about an hour, he crossed the trail between the two villages and continued on to the southeast. Since shortly before dark, there had been a lot of noise, mostly whooping and hollering coming from the camp. Crazy Runner's curiosity got the best of him and he crawled over to see what was going on.

In the camp, he saw two men in French uniforms handing out jugs of whiskey to the Indians. Big Jim had told him that both the French and English would get the Indians drunk because it made them easier to control.

While he was watching the Indians, the clouds broke and the moon started shining bright. Crazy Runner knew this would make it easier for him to travel, but also easier for the Creek to see him, so he left immediately heading southeast.

He had just gotten out of sight of the camp's fire when he got to a little ridge and saw the fires in two more camps, one southeast and one south. It seemed that the Creek had one large village and many smaller camps in all directions.

Crazy Runner changed his direction and headed east. He came across a well-worn path that seemed to connect the camp to the southeast and the main village. He got past that trail just as the sky was beginning to get light, but the sun was not yet visible.

Since this is the time of day when most men, Indians or white, are just beginning to stir, Crazy Runner felt it was a good time to put some distance between him and the Creek camps. He started running at full speed. If he had time, he could have stopped at several places and killed a deer as he saw many.

Each time he came to a hill, he would pause and check out everything all around him. About noon, when he had stopped to check out the area, he saw three groups of Creek, each only a couple of miles away. One was heading in the same direction, southeast, a second group was heading east and the third group was heading south. They were either hunting or scouting. It did not matter, because they were between him and his destination.

Crazy Runner decided to take a nap. He had not slept in a day and a half. With this many Creek around he might need his rest for a long run. He found a well-hidden place and lay down. He was asleep almost immediately. When he awoke it was full dark, he started to the southeast.

He had seen the signs of the Creeks in the moonlight. He was walking and not running, but being very cautious. After about two hours, he saw a campfire directly in front of him. He circled to the east around the campfire. At one point, he was on a rise and with his telescope was able to see that it was one of the group of Creeks.

At dawn, he came to a clearing. It was very large, almost ½ mile across. It would take him almost an hour to go around the clearing. He stepped out a little into the clearing and used his telescope to look in every direction. He saw nothing. He took out running. In three steps, he was at full speed. He had gotten about halfway across the clearing when an arrow landed to his right. Without slowing down, he looked behind him and saw three more arrows in the ground. There were four Creek shooting at him. Two of the Creek had taken out after him and the other two were in the process of shooting arrows at him again. He saw the direction the arrows were coming and slightly altered his direction so they stuck harmlessly in the ground. Then those two also started after him.

The time for being careful was past, now was the time for speed. He was across the clearing before the first two Creek had even gotten halfway across, so he knew he already had about a quarter-mile lead.

A thought suddenly came to his head. Should he get far enough ahead to find a hiding spot and then kill them in the same way Big Jim had taught him with the Shawnee (kill the last one first) or should he keep running. By running, that was making a lot of noise and he might run into more Creek braves.

He topped a hill and saw that the mountain he was headed for was not that far now. Running at this speed, he could reach it in three to four hours. He knew that mountain was the edge of Creek territory and once he was on that mountain he would be in Cherokee territory.

He came to a stream and stopped to get a drink of water. Then he took off. Because he was in the trees he could only see the Creek following him occasionally, but he could hear them. His lead continually increased. He figured that if his lead were enough to where they could no longer see him they would probably stop.

After about an hour, they did stop, but Crazy Runner did not. He kept running until he was to the mountain and started up. He continued up the mountain walking and when he got to the top, he looked back and could no longer see the Creek braves.

When he looked at the valley, he realized he was at the

northwestern end of it. Using his telescope, he could see the Settlement House and a couple of cabins. Hank Jacobs had not wasted any time.

CHAPTER 27—WARNING THE SETTLERS

The valley was divided into three parts. The northwestern part had a mountain on the north and west and rivers on the east and south sides. The northeastern part, where the Settlement House was located, had mountains on the north and east sides and rivers on the south and west. The southern part had a river on the north side and mountains on the other three sides.

Crazy Runner headed down toward where the two rivers intersected. He was hoping that the settlers would send a raft over the river to pick him up. It took him two hours to reach the river. The settlers must have had a lookout, because as soon as he came through the foliage into the open at the riverbank he saw several well-armed settlers across the river.

He immediately waved at them and yelled, "Could someone come over and pick me up?" Before two long two men appeared carrying a canoe. One of them got in the canoe and paddled over to the Crazy Runner, picked him up and returned to the east shore.

Everyone immediately started shaking his hand and patting

him on the back. As soon as Crazy Runner saw Hank Jacobs he said, "There is a big problem. I need to meet with all of you."

Jacobs led him, with the others following, to the Settlement House. When they got there, Jacobs rang a bell. Within 30 minutes, all of the settlers were present outside the Settlement House. Crazy Runner said quietly to Hank, "I don't think the children should hear what I have to say." Hank Jacobs went over to a couple of women and they quietly got all of the children and went down to the riverbank.

Crazy Runner walked in the door of the Settlement House and was amazed. There was one big room and three smaller rooms on the east side on the first floor. On the west wall was the largest fireplace Crazy Runner had ever seen; it was about five feet tall and ten feet wide. The second floor had an open hallway around the building and the hallway was about ten feet wide. All of the windows were on the second floor. Hank Jacobs led Crazy Runner up a ladder to the second floor.

At one corner they stopped and Hank Jacobs told him, "Everyone is here, what do you want to tell us?"

"The French are wanting to get the settlers out of Kentucky. They are using the Indians to wage war on the settlers to scare them out or to kill them. In the north they are using the Seneca and down in this area they are using the Creek. They are paying them one Franc for each scalp they collect.

You have an advantage in that you are in Cherokee territory and the Creek do not want to chance a war with the Cherokee and the white settlers at the same time. I figure that if they do decide to attack you they will be more likely to come by water than over the mountain."

Hank Jacobs said, "First of all, we have already had some French come into the valley from the west on the river. They did not get far before we confronted them. The French told us to beware of the Indians because they were on the warpath. We told them that this was Cherokee land and they had promised us protection. They immediately turned around and left.

Secondly, we have developed an alarm system. Follow me."

Hank went around to the east side of the second floor and Crazy Runner followed him up a ladder and out on to the roof. There was another ladder attached to the roof and leading up to a box-like area on the roof. The area was big enough for six men. There was a waist high wall all around with a hole in the floor for someone to enter from the ladder and there was a roof on it to protect the people from the weather or arrows.

Hank said to the man there, "Signal."

The man picked up a limb with a piece of white cloth tied to one end. He faced to the north, extended the limb out and up and waived it. Hank had quietly pointed to the tallest part of the mountain. Before long, a flag from that point waived back.

Hank said, "That is how we knew you were coming without anything noisy to alert you that we knew you were coming. From that point, a person can see all of both rivers and all of the ridges in each direction. We have worked out a signal system to tell us when someone is coming and from where they are coming.

We have a system where a man is in both of these posts day and night. At night the man on the mountain uses a lantern to signal if necessary.

We know that several times the Cherokee have come and spied on us to see what we are doing. We never confronted them. They were here two or three times before they realized that we knew they were there. Since it is all defensive and not offensive they seemed okay with it."

Crazy Runner replied, "The Cherokee have a similar system, only they use bird noises or arrows, depending on the distance.

After we left here, Big Jim and I went to the Cherokee. They already knew you were building this Settlement House and they thought that was smart and the Chief will be here to meet you when warmer weather comes."

"That is good," Hank said as he started down the ladder. When they got down to the ground level, he asked Crazy Runner, "Where is Big Jim?"

"We came across a settlement the Creeks had burned it to the ground. He had led those people to that area over a year ago. One woman and five children had hidden and escaped. He took them to another settlement he had guided people to in the opposite direction and I came to warn you, but I see that wasn't necessary."

Chapter 28—Christmas

Crazy Runner spent the night in the Settlement House. It was very comfortable. The next morning he arose and started packing up his things. Hank Jacobs walked up to him and said, "You can't leave now, this is Christmas Eve!" Crazy Runner did not even realize it was December. Hank continued, "We have a lot to be thankful for and you are a part of that. Please stay until at least after Christmas."

"I will be happy to." Crazy Runner said.

People all through the settlement had put everything else on hold for these two days. The plans were for a big two-day celebration. The men had hunted for all types of meat in the last few days. The women were fixing the food. They planned on five consecutive large meals, beginning with the noon meal on Christmas Eve day.

The men had found a salt lick in the valley so it was easy to preserve the meat. They had built a large root cellar next to the Settlement House for the entire settlement to share.

During the morning, using one of their canoes, Crazy Runner

was able to cross the rivers and he ran all over the valley floor. He found where the settlers had put stakes in the ground to mark where they were going to build their cabins. They had finished the Settlement House and eight cabins in the time that he had been gone.

Hank Jacobs had the settlers draw lots to determine the order in which people would have their cabin built. Then all of the men would work together to build the cabins in that order. They would first clear the land and then with the lumber that had been cut, they would build the cabin. The larger the family, then the larger cabin they would receive. They only had three more cabins to build and every family would have their own home. They would follow the same procedure for clearing the farmland for plowing.

When he arrived back at the Settlement House, they were just about to start lunch. There was a prayer and then everyone filed by some long tables with all of the food set up. Each person would take what they wanted and find a place to sit down and then eat. There was a lot of pleasant conversation as people ate.

After lunch, the women and children cleaned things up and several men took off with axes. Another two hours passed before they came back carrying a very large pine tree. They nailed two pieces of wood to the bottom of the tree and then carried it into the Settlement House. They tied four ropes around the tree about ten feet from the bottom. They walked the tree upright in the center of the room and threw the ropes to men on each side of the second floor who tied it off on the second floor railings.

The rest of the day was spent in making homemade decorations, singing Christmas carols, visiting, and eating. Everyone, including those who already had completed cabins spent the night in the Settlement House. After all of the children were asleep several adults slipped out to come back later with gifts for the children. It had been planned so that each child in the settlement would get the same number of gifts. These gifts were placed under the tree.

Christmas morning, as soon as the first child woke up and saw the gifts under the tree, he made so much noise that everyone woke up. The sun was not even up yet. The children immediately found their gifts and opened them with the adults proudly observing. Then the women started breakfast as everyone sang Christmas Carols. Before breakfast, Hank Jacobs gave a long prayer and in that prayer, he mentioned Crazy Runner and Big Jim. To Crazy Runner's memory this was the first time anyone had mentioned him in a prayer.

The lookout schedule had been modified so that instead on one person being on duty for six straight hours, they were only on duty for two hours at a time so each could spend more time with their families at Christmas.

The rest of the day was spent relaxing and visiting. Crazy Runner had never known happiness like he was now witnessing. He felt honored to be a part of it.

Chapter 29—Kithuhwa

The next day when things returned to normal in the settlement, Crazy Runner decided to head to Kithuhwa. The Cherokee in that village were the first ones who had treated him as well as the people in this settlement and he wanted to spend some more time there. He also wanted to warn them about what the French were doing.

He knew the country so he ran. He ran across the valley, up the mountain on the east side and continued running most of the day. He stopped for the night in the second Cherokee village he had come to. At the end of the second day of running, he came to Kithuhwa.

Crazy Runner immediately went to the lodge of Running Bear. Running Bear was delighted to see him and immediately wanted him to tell about all of his exploits. Crazy Runner told him about traveling all the way to the Big River in the west and back. He told also about his run-in with the Shawnee and his running the gauntlet. Meeting Big Jim and leading the settlers to the Cherokee land was the next portion of his history and he was proud to show Running Bear his tomahawk and telescope. Running Bear had seen men looking through telescopes before, but this was the first time he had ever had a chance to look through one and it amazed him.

Then Crazy Runner told Running Bear about the French using the Seneca and Creeks to make war on the white settlers. Running Bear told him that Crazy Runner must tell the chiefs this news. There were Englishmen in the camp who were trying to convince the Cherokee to war against the French and Spanish to the south and southwest.

Later that night Running Bear left the lodge with Crazy Runner there and went to speak to the chiefs. A short time later, he returned and asked Crazy Runner to come with him. They went to the large lodge and all of the elders who had been there when he passed his tests were there, plus a few more. Crazy Runner started to tell them in Cherokee, but he was having problems with some of the words since it had been several months since he had spoken Cherokee. Running Bear told him to start over and tell it in English and he would translate it.

Crazy Runner said, "With my own eyes I have seen Frenchmen leading the Creek against the Shawnee and white settlers. I have also seen Frenchmen leading the Seneca against white settlers. Some of the Frenchmen doing this are traders, but most are French soldiers. I have found out that the Frenchmen are paying one French Franc for each white scalp the Creeks and Seneca can take."

Crazy Runner was told by one of the chiefs, in good English, "The English have offered us one English pound for each French or Spanish scalp."

Crazy Runner asked, "The great Cherokee Nation does not kill for the money like the white man do they? Are not the

Cherokee more civilized than the white man? Would not taking scalps for money violate Cherokee law?"

The chiefs were silent for some time, just looking from one to the other. Then one said, "Crazy Runner has said some wise things that we must consider. We thank you for your information."

Crazy Runner and Running Bear went back to Running Bear's lodge for the evening.

The next morning a brave came up and handed Crazy Runner a piece of paper. It was a poster that read, "Runaway White Slave, answers to the name of Crazy Runner, $500 reward, see Thomas Cook at Violet Plantation." The brave told him these posters were all around the area to the southeast and east. Running Bear told Crazy Runner that he knew about the posters, but he also knew that no one had ever come looking for him on Cherokee land. He also said, "No Cherokee would ever turn in any man for the white man's money, especially a brother." They shook hands.

In the afternoon, Crazy Runner and Running Bear went hunting. Running Bear was very impressed at how skilled Crazy Runner had become at tracking game. He was also impressed with his ability to bring down a deer with his bow and arrow, instead of using his rifle.

Crazy Runner told him about Big Jim and all of the things that he had learned from Big Jim. Running Bear laughed when Crazy Runner told about his first encounter with ice. Running Bear had not seen ice, but he had seen snow.

It was hard to tell who was enjoying this time together more, Crazy Runner or Running Bear. Crazy Runner thought of Running Bear as the father he never knew and Running Bear thought of Crazy Runner as the son he had never had.

CHAPTER 30—CHICKASAW

Two days later, a brave came running into the village and went immediately to the large lodge. Another brave came out of the large lodge and ran around the village gathering the chiefs. They all went back into the large lodge.

About five minutes passed before the chiefs came out of the large lodge and Crazy Runner was summoned. When he arrived at the large lodge he was told by one of the chiefs, "You are the fastest runner. We need you to go the four villages to the north and the three to the west. Tell them that the Chickasaw have attacked our village to the southwest. They are to send some braves to join us in the attack on the Chickasaw and have the rest search for others around their villages who might want to attack the Cherokee."

Crazy Runner ran back to Running Bears lodge, gathered his things and quickly started on this mission. It took him two and a half days to go to all seven villages, give them the message and return to Kithuhwa.

When he returned Running Bear told him that the war chief

and braves had left the same day he had. Crazy Runner ate, slept for about four hours, and then started after the braves to join in the fight. Since the braves were walking, he caught up to them shortly before dawn.

He immediately told the war chief that the other villages had been notified. They fed him and then they started toward the village. When they were about an hour from the village, scouts were sent out in every direction as the rest proceeded with caution.

Just as they were within eyesight of the village, a shot was heard from the south. The chief gave a hand signal and the Cherokee braves scattered in all directions in groups of six to eight, but most of the groups went toward the south. Crazy Runner was not sure what to do, so he stayed with the war chief. Crazy Runner assumed that the scout to the south had discovered there was a trap and fired his rifle to warn the others. That probably meant forfeiting his own life for the good of the tribe.

The war chief noticed Crazy Runner looking at the village with his telescope and asked, "What do you see?"

"Many dead people, men, women and children."

The war chief then said, "Go to that ridge and climb that tall tree. See what you can see with your telescope and come tell me."

Crazy Runner ran at full speed and was climbing the tree in ten minutes. When he got as high as he dare climb he first looked in all directions with his eye and saw the Cherokee, but no one else. Then when he looked to the south with the telescope, he could see many Chickasaw hiding in ambush on a hill above the village. While looking around he saw another large group of Chickasaw hiding in a gully to the west side of the village.

Crazy Runner did not remember all of the Cherokee hand

signals so he just waved his hands and motioned for the Cherokee war chief to come towards him. He climbed down and immediately ran full speed to meet the war chief.

"There are two large groups of Chickasaw. One group is on the hill on the south side of the village and the other is in the low area on the west side of the village."

At about the same time a large number of Cherokee braves came up from the other villages that Crazy Runner had gone to tell. The war chief sent some to the north to go around the village to get behind those in the gully. The rest followed the war chief toward the village.

Now Crazy Runner understood the strategy. The braves who had come from Kithuhwa were circling around to the south to get behind the Chickasaw on the south hill because the war chief trusted the braves from the other villages would be there. One group of braves was going behind those in the gulley. The war chief was going the lead the rest directly into the trap, but actually, it would be the Chickasaw who were trapped with Cherokee both in front and behind them.

The war chief made a hand signal and the Cherokee braves started making noise. They were noisily stomping on the ground. When they got to about 50 yards from the village, they started whooping and hollering. Crazy Runner thought this did not make much sense. Then he realized that this noise would cover any noise the others were making in sneaking behind the Chickasaw and direct the full attention of the Chickasaw toward the noise. The war chief kept them at the edge of the clearing with most of the braves in the woods. This was an old Indian trick for hoping the enemy, if he were around, would show himself. The war chief knew the Chickasaw knew this trick, but what he was doing was keeping all of the attention on him while the others got into position.

Crazy Runner had no idea how many Chickasaw there were. Since they were in hiding, he figured he had seen about thirty braves and there were probably about thirty more that he did not see. However, with the arrival of the braves from the other villages the Cherokee had more than 100.

After about 15 minutes, the war chief led braves into the camp. Only about 30 braves entered the camp with him. Crazy Runner and 20 more braves were hidden in the brush just outside the clearing. The first group of braves immediately started checking the bodies of the persons in the camp to make sure all were dead. About five minutes after they started doing this the sky was filled with arrows flying towards the village. The war chief yelled something and the braves in the village immediately ran to the outskirts of the village with only one brave being hit by an arrow.

The Chickasaw started their attack from both the south and west. As soon as they made themselves visible, Crazy Runner and the 20 braves with him rushed into the clearing. The Cherokee who had taken up positions behind the Chickasaw waited until the Chickasaw were close to the village and then they started attacking.

One Chickasaw was aiming his rifle at the war chief, but Crazy Runner shot him first. Crazy Runner started to load his rifle, but he did not have time. A Chickasaw was coming toward him at full speed, while he was tamping down the charge, wad, and ball with his ramrod. He aimed the rifle at the brave and fired; the long ramrod went right through the Indian. Another brave was coming towards him so he killed him with a pistol shot. He hit a fourth brave in the head with his rifle, which knocked him down, and then he buried his tomahawk in the brave's chest.

Crazy Runner pulled his tomahawk out and looked around

with his tomahawk in his left hand and his knife in his right hand. The battle was just about over. A few Chickasaw had escaped, but most were dead.

Only fourteen Cherokee braves had been killed and ten more injured.

The war chief and about 70 braves started out to the southwest. Crazy Runner was told to stay in this village to help with the dead and wounded, then return to Kithuhwa.

Crazy Runner found the ramrod for his rifle, but it was bent. He would have to wait until he got back to the village to repair it.

After the dead were given a proper burial ceremony then Crazy Runner and the others headed back to Kithuhwa. When they arrived back at the village, Crazy Runner asked Running Bear, who had not left Kithuhwa, "Where did the war chief and the braves go?"

Running Bear replied, "To achieve balance in the world."

Crazy Runner thought about this and then realized what they were doing.

CHAPTER 31—A-WI U-S-DI

Four days later, the war chief and braves returned. In the retaliation raid, only four Cherokee had been killed, but an entire Chickasaw village had been wiped out. They had also burned the village and the dead in it. This was the ultimate insult to the Chickasaw, because the Chickasaw believed their spirit must stay on earth if their body were burned. At the same time, it sent a very strong message to the Chickasaw about what would happen if they ever attacked the Cherokee again.

As a result of this battle, Crazy Runner had easily figured out that the main reasons that the Cherokee won their battles was because they had superior strategy and they never went into a battle with only a few braves.

Several braves had seen him kill the four Chickasaw in the battle. For this, Running Bear had told him, they would make him a warrior. For this ceremony, he must have a nice set of buckskins to wear.

Running Bear took Crazy Runner to a lodge and told him that he was to go in and the women in there would make him two sets of buckskins, one for ceremonies and one for everyday wear. Crazy Runner went in and saw three older women. All three immediately started putting him in different positions and measuring with string his size in all areas. One put a piece of string around his neck and then tied it so that it retained the size and then she did the same thing to his chest. Another did the same thing with his waist and thighs. The third was measuring the length of this arms and legs. After they got all of the measurements, they ushered him out.

After he left that lodge, Running Bear took him to another lodge. Both of them went in and Crazy Runner immediately noticed how hot it was. Running Bear started removing his clothes and he told Crazy Runner to do the same. There were many hot rocks in the center of the lodge. It did not take long before they were both sweating. Crazy Runner had never been this hot before.

After an hour, Running Bear pulled a very large container of water out and told Crazy Runner to wash himself. Crazy Runner watched Running Bear wash his hair and then spread the water all over his body and he did the same.

When they finished, they got dressed and went back to the lodge with the three women. Crazy Runner went in and the three women had buckskin material that they held up to him in different places to see if it was the right size, then they sent him out.

Running Bear then took him to the war chief who explained the ceremony that would happen that night. When this was finished, he went back to the three women.

Almost as soon as he went into the lodge, the women motioned for him to take off his clothes. When he just stood there, one of the women yelled something he did not understand. Running Bear, who was standing outside, started laughing and said to Crazy Runner from outside, "You had better take off your clothes yourself. She just said if you don't they will do it for you and then kick you out of the lodge naked."

Crazy Runner quickly took off his clothes. The women gave him some pants to put on first. The length on the legs was a little long so they made him take them off and one woman started working on that while the other two had him put on a shirt. It fit fine. It did not take long for the woman to finish his pants. They fit fine. He really liked the feel of the buckskins; they were the nicest clothes he had ever had.

One of the women told him to sit down and started looking at his hair. She said something to another woman who left and returned a little later with a girl. The girl stood behind Crazy Runner and started running things through his hair. It hurt. His hair had not been combed since he had left the plantation. The girl explained to him, in good English, "You must look nice for the ceremony. Your hair is tangled, so I must comb out the tangles. You are supposed to be very brave. If that is so, why do you yell when a girl pulls your hair?"

Crazy Runner laughed, "What is your name?"

"A-wi U-s-di, it means Little Deer. My mother said you were very embarrassed at taking off your clothes in front of the old women, why is that? We women care for you as babies, don't we? We bear your children, don't we?"

"I guess so," Crazy Runner said, very embarrassed. Then Little Deer laughed. Crazy Runner had not really noticed her when she came in because he was watching the women working on his ceremony buckskins. Little Deer was completely behind him and he could not see her at all. She had a nice sounding voice; Crazy Runner wondered what she looked like.

He asked, "Where did you learn to speak English so well?"

"I learned from some of the people in the village like Running Bear."

It took over an hour for Little Deer to get all of the tangles out of his hair. When she finished she said, "You need to comb your hair once a day to make sure it does not get like that again."

Crazy Runner stood and turned to face her. She was short. The top of her head did not quite reach his shoulders. She had long black hair and pretty black eyes. She was very pleasing to look at.

One of the old women said something. Crazy Runner did not understand. Little Deer told him, "She wants you to take off these clothes so you can try on your ceremonial ones."

Crazy Runner embarrassingly said, "Right now?"

Little Deer laughed and said, "I will leave".

The ceremonial clothes fit perfectly and also felt extremely comfortable. They had little strings of beads hanging from the sides of the legs and arms. There was also a small picture on the chest of a man running, which had been sown in beads.

He was told he must change back into the regular buckskins because he was not to be seen in the ceremonial dress while the sun was still up. Once again, he took off all of his clothes and put on the first set of buckskins. The women motioned that he was to leave his original clothes here. Then he carried the ceremonial clothes to Running Bear's lodge.

Chapter 32—The Ceremony

As the sun set a big fire was started in the center of the large circle in the middle of the village. Running Bear had already changed into his ceremonial clothes. Crazy Runner was to carry his clothes to the big lodge and after a small ceremony there, he was to put them on.

When he went into the big lodge he saw all of the chiefs were already there. Running Bear instructed him to go stand in the center. The medicine man then danced around him, giving a chant and waving some feathers above Crazy Runners head. Then Running Bear came up with Crazy Runner's ceremonial clothes. After Crazy Runner had changed clothes, the medicine man repeated the earlier process.

Crazy Runner heard the drums, and then he followed the chiefs to the circle in the middle of the camp. The entire village was already standing in a large circle. All of the chiefs sat and then Crazy Runner sat in the place the war chief had earlier told him to sit, which was to his right. One of the old women who had helped make his two new outfits came forward carrying his hold clothes and three them into the fire.

The warriors started dancing around the fire. They were very graceful in the way they danced. Crazy Runner hoped that some day he would be taught how to dance like that.

As the warriors were dancing, the women of the village served food to those sitting with Little Deer serving Crazy Runner. Once he saw her, he had trouble taking his eyes off her. His eyes followed her to where she was going. The war chief hit him on his arm to get his attention back to the dancing.

Crazy Runner smiled and intently watched the dancing, sneaking occasional peeks at Little Deer. Whenever he looked at her, he saw that she was always looking at him. After the chiefs and Crazy Runner were finished eating, the dancing suddenly stopped and the warriors sat behind the chiefs around the circle. The war chief stood and the medicine man brought him a headband with one feather in it. Crazy Runner rose to his knees and the war chief placed the headband on his head. Then Crazy Runner stood up and walked around the campfire and whenever he walked in front of anyone, they would whoop and holler.

When he had made one complete circle around the fire he returned to where he had been sitting, bowed to the war chief, and then sat down behind the war chief in the second circle of warriors. As soon as he was seated there was more cheering and that signaled the end of the ceremony.

Crazy Runner was now a Cherokee warrior.

CHAPTER 33—CHALLENGE

The next morning Crazy Runner was walking around the village when a brave came up to him and threw a knife that stuck in the ground between his feet. Crazy Runner had seen this brave around, but did not know his name. He picked up the knife and threw it back sticking it in the ground between the feet of the brave.

Several people had watched this exchange and suddenly a lot of whooping and hollering began. Crazy Runner had no idea what was going on so he walked back to Running Bear's lodge to ask him.

Running Bear said, "When he threw the knife between your feet he was challenging you to a fight to the death. When you picked up the knife and threw it back at his feet, you were accepting the challenge."

"Why? I don't even know him."

"I will find out. You stay in the lodge until I return."

When Running Bear returned he told Crazy Runner, "It was Angry Wolf who challenged you. Last night at the ceremony, you were watching Little Deer and she was watching you. Angry Wolf wants to marry Little Deer. He has been gathering up items to give her father. He must do that so her father will give him permission. In our ways that means she belongs to him, unless she changes her mind. Angry Wolf figures she can't change her mind if you are dead."

Crazy Runner said, "So if I die, then he gets to marry Little Deer. What happens if I kill him?"

"Then you must marry Little Deer! How did you and Little Deer meet?"

"Her mother brought her in yesterday to comb my hair. I was in the lodge with the three women and her. She spoke very good English, so we talked a little in English. Almost all of the time we were talking she was standing behind me. That is all that happened, until last night.

When she brought me my food, she looked very pretty and gave me a big smile and I smiled back and said, 'Thank you'. I then watched her until the war chief tapped me on the arm and motioned for me to pay attention to the dancing. I looked at her a couple of more times, but I said nothing."

Running Bear asked, "If you win the fight, are you willing to stay here and settle down and raise a family?"

"No, I want to travel. But, I will not run away from a fight."

Running Bear said, "I will explain this to Angry Wolf and see if I can get him to withdraw his challenge."

When Running Bear returned he said, "He understands that you may not have meant anything by what you did, but since he has challenged you, he must go through with it or lose face."

"So I have to fight him or run away in the middle of the night and never come back. Are those my only choices?" Crazy Runner asked.

"Yes."

"What if I win, do I have to marry Little Deer?"

"You will have won the right to pay her father for permission to marry her."

"What is Angry Wolf supposed to pay?"

"Five bear skins and two rifles. That is a very high price."

"What if I don't have that, then her father will not give me his permission to marry her."

"That is correct. But you will then be shamed and no other father will allow you to marry their daughter, when you do decide to settle down."

"How does this challenge work?"

"A long rope is tied to both of your ankles and you each have your knives. You fight until one of you is dead."

Crazy Runner did not sleep well that night thinking about the fight and wondering what to do about the situation if he won the fight.

The challenge was to take place shortly after dawn on the outskirts of the camp in a meadow. On the way there, Crazy Runner asked Running Bear, if Angry Wolf understood English.

Running Bear answered, "A little."

When they got to the meadow, Crazy Runner noticed Little Deer standing up front next to the war chief. He asked, "Why is she standing next to the war chief?"

"Little Deer is his daughter."

Crazy Runner, thinking very quickly, said, "Does he know that I saved his life in the fight with the Chickasaw?"

"Yes."

"Because I saved his life, doesn't he owe a debt to me, to achieve balance?"

"Yes, that is true."

Crazy Runner headed directly toward the war chief, with Running Bear following. Crazy Runner said to Running Bear,

"Tell him exactly what I say. Tell him that I saved his life and he owes me a balance of life. What I want from him in repayment is for him to allow Angry Wolf to marry Little Deer with whatever gifts Angry Wolf already has."

Running Bear looked puzzled and then repeated it. Little Bear looked just a little disappointed that maybe two men would not be fighting over her. The war chief took several minutes to think this over and then he nodded 'yes' and signaled Angry Wolf to come over.

The war chief told Angry Wolf that Little Deer was his because of what Crazy Runner had done. This satisfied Angry Wolf and the challenge was ended.

As they were leaving the meadow, Crazy Runner said to Running Bear, "I am glad that worked out. I was not looking forward to killing him."

Running Bear replied, "You are the lucky one. I did not tell you earlier, but Angry Wolf has killed three others in challenges."

CHAPTER 34—TRAVELING AGAIN

The next morning Crazy Runner packed up his things and left the village. He explained to Running Bear, "I do not want to cause anyone any trouble. If I am gone for some time, then people should forget this act and just concentrate on me in the future. Besides, I am getting in a traveling mood again."

Running Bear understood.

Crazy Runner had not seen any of the country to the south or southwest. However, there were wanted posters out on him to the south and the Chickasaw were to the southwest. Considering the Cherokee attack on the Chickasaw village Crazy Runner calculated that it would not be a good time to be traveling in that direction. Therefore, he decided to head due west as there was territory in that direction he had not yet seen.

Crazy Runner did a lot of running whenever possible. This new direction was tough because there were constant hills and mountains and very few ridges to follow for a long distance.

He knew these types of mountains would be a good place to find bears. Because it was still winter, most of the bears would still be hibernating. He just had to be careful about staying out of those places where bears might be. Crazy Runner knew that many Indians did their bear hunting at this time of year. The bears were less active and easier to kill. He had to look out for Indians who were bear hunting.

These mountains were so rugged with very few areas large enough for a village so that meant he should not have to worry about a Creek or Chickasaw village. Running Bear had told him that these mountains divided the Creek and Chickasaw territories.

On days where the sun was out and the sky clear Crazy Runner could see for many miles. On many occasions he would simple sit on a rock with his telescope and carefully look in all directions. He was able to see many majestic waterfalls. In the far distance to the north and south of several lookout points, he was able to see some Indian villages.

About two weeks on the trail, he started noticing signs of someone who was in front of him and making his way along the top of the mountains. This person was traveling barefoot and not attempting to hide his trail.

Crazy Runner was sure that this was neither a trapper nor an Indian. Neither would be barefoot in the mountains. Since this person was going in the same direction, Crazy Runner decided to keep going but just be more careful. He had been following him for two days before the trail started being fresh.

CHAPTER 35—SLAVE

At the end of the third day of following the trail, he caught sight of the man. He was a black man. To Crazy Runner this meant that the man was an escaped slave. Crazy Runner had never met or heard of any black man who was not a slave.

Crazy Runner watched him make camp about an hour before dark. The man was careful to gather dry wood and pick a place for a fire where the light from the fire would not show for a long distance.

Crazy Runner decided to go around the man and wait for him somewhere ahead of him. This man was frightened and therefore he must be careful how he approached him.

He found a place about a mile west of the camp. The man would travel through a narrow gorge about ¼ mile long. Crazy Runner waited behind a large boulder for him. Shortly before dawn, a good-sized deer came along and Crazy Runner killed it with his bow and arrow. He hung up the deer on a limb to bleed out so that when the man came out of the gorge he would see it about 50 feet ahead of him.

CRAZY RUNNER - TRAILBLAZER - 1750

The man came through the gorge in about an hour. As soon as he was through the gorge, he spotted the deer hanging from the tree. He stopped and carefully looked around in every direction. When he did not see anyone the man slowly approached the deer. As he did, Crazy Runner stepped out from behind the large boulder, got into the open behind the man, and stopped.

The black man was about about two inches shorter and about twenty pounds heavier than Crazy Runner. He looked to be about ten years older than Crazy Runner.

Crazy Runner then said, "The deer has many uses. One is to eat and another is to provide clothing." The man was completely startled. Immediately he looked around in every direction. Crazy Runner said, "I mean you no harm. The deerskin can be used to make you some moccasins so the traveling on the rocks will be easier."

"Who are you?" the man said.

"I am called Crazy Runner. What is your name?"

"They calls me Sam. I heared of you. You is an escaped slave also."

"That is simply a misunderstanding. Where are you going?"

"Ohio."

"You are heading in the wrong direction. You are heading west and Ohio is north. Let's get some deer meat in you and then make you some moccasins. Do you know how to skin a deer?"

"Yas, sir."

Crazy Runner gave him his knife and then proceeded to get some wood for a fire. About the time, the fire was going good the deer had been skinned. Sam started cooking the deer meat, while Crazy Runner stretched the deer skin between two trees.

As they sat down and ate, Crazy Runner asked, "Why are you trying to get to Ohio?"

"The mastah sold my wife and chillin' to a man in Ohio. I am going to find them."

In the discussions that followed, Sam told Crazy Runner that his parents had been captured in Africa and brought over to Carolina on a slave ship. He had been born on that slave ship. Both of his parents had died on that slave ship. Crazy Runner realized that Sam and he had a lot in common. Sam had been married for six years to another slave on the same plantation that he had lived on for his entire life. He had two sons, one five-years-old and one three-years-old, and two daughters, one four and one two. The Master had sold the wife and four children to a man who ran a plantation in Ohio.

Crazy Runner said, "Ohio is a very big place, how do you expect to find her?"

"The man said he has a plantation where the Ohio and Allegheny Rivers meet."

"I know where that is. I will take you there."

Chapter 36—Heading North

They spent the next day in the camp preparing for the journey. They cooked all of the deer meat. The place where Crazy Runner had stretched the deerskin had strong winds that lasted all night long, by morning the deerskin was dry. Crazy Runner made a pair of moccasins for Sam and the rest of the deerskin was for Sam to use to wrap around himself since they were heading north. Sam had told Crazy Runner that he was not a fast runner, but he could run a very long distance without tiring.

During the day, Crazy Runner told Sam about the trouble with the Indians and they would be traveling through Creek and Shawnee territory. He taught Sam how to travel quiet and not to leave signs where they had been. The deer meat would last them for several days.

It took an entire day to get down out of the mountains. The land here was not flat, but it was not rocky and allowed for more rapid movement. The next day they started out running trying to follow animal trails whenever possible. Crazy Runner ran fast, but not full speed and Sam was able to keep up with him. They ran for about three hours and then stopped at a stream to drink and rest.

When both were rested, they crossed the stream and continued running. About two hours later Crazy Runner stopped, knelt down and closely examined the ground. Sam remembered what Crazy Runner had said on the mountain that whenever Crazy Runner stopped abruptly to stop also and not say anything.

Crazy Runner stood up and whispered, "Creek". Then they left the trail and slowly headed off through the brush in a northeasterly direction. They were walking on fallen trees whenever possible so they would not leave a trail. When they had gone about a mile, they came to another animal trail. Crazy Runner examined it and then started slowly following it. After a while, they started running again and ran for the rest of the day.

At sundown, they found a good place to spend the night that had a lot of heavy brush to block the wind. They could not risk a fire, but with the wind blocked, they spent a comfortable night.

At sunrise, they continued traveling north. They started walking until Crazy Runner was sure there were no signs of Indians on the trail, and then they continued running. They ran all morning and shortly after noon came to a small river where they stopped to rest and eat.

They were ready to continue when Crazy Runner heard something. He motioned for Sam to follow him. They entered the river and slowly went downstream about 50 yards and got into some brush on the same side and lay quietly. About ten minutes later a dozen Creek crossed the river from the same side they were on to the east side.

They lay there quietly for some time. Sam whispered to Crazy Runner, "How did you know they were coming?"

"Something a friend taught me, the birds in that direction stopped making noise."

They continued north staying on the west side of the river. After an hour, they started running again. Close to sundown, they came to a high ridge and Crazy Runner could see many miles to the southeast the mountains that were on the west side of the valley with Hank Jacobs and the settlers. From now on most of the country they would be in would be familiar to Crazy Runner.

They found a place out of the wind and made camp for the night.

Chapter 37—Wolves

The next morning they started to the northeast. Crazy Runner knew there were a lot more Creek in this area so they changed their traveling. They would run for a half-hour and walk for an hour. In this manner they would cover more ground than just walking, would be more observant of their surroundings, and have the energy for a good long run should they get chased by the Creek.

In mid-afternoon, they came to a river, crossed it and continued northeast. They found a second river and staying back from the river about fifty feet they continued north on the west side of the river, Crazy Runner was sure that this was the same river that the Hank Jacobs group had traveled down, only he was now on the opposite side.

They found an empty cave, gathered some wood, and spent a nice warm night. During the night, Crazy Runner was awakened by the sound of wolves howling. He went to the entrance of the cave and looked out. There he saw the large white wolf he had seen many months before. The white wolf was still leading a pack of wolves. This was the largest pack of wolves he had ever heard anyone mention. He was able to count twelve, but he could hear more off in a short distance.

Crazy Runner gathered some more wood and built up the fire inside the cave. Sam was still sleeping soundly. With a bright fire, the wolves would not enter the cave. At least they were safe until the fire went out. Crazy Runner went back to sleep. He was not worried since he did sleep lightly.

Sam woke up and started out of the cave. Crazy Runner said, "I would not do that if I were you. There is a pack of wolves just outside the cave entrance."

"What are we going to do?"

"We are going to wait until full light and then I have a plan."

After the sun was up, Crazy Runner got out his bow. He stayed far enough back in the cave to where the light did not catch him. He shot one wolf. The other wolves started sniffing the dead one. Crazy Runner then shot a second wolf. This time the wolves took off heading north. Crazy Runner waited until they were out of sight and then he and Sam bolted out of the cave heading east toward the river.

When they got to the river, the water was up and running swiftly so they could not cross at this point. They started north running along the river's edge. They had been running for about a mile when Crazy Runner heard the wolves again. They were on a ridge to the west and headed down toward them. It appeared that there were about 20 of them. The river was behind them to the east, flat lands were to the south, and there was a high rock wall to the north beside the waterfalls.

Crazy Runner handed Sam the tomahawk and told him to run for the rocks as fast as he could and climb as fast as he could. Sam, who was behind Crazy Runner, found the trail the Indians used to get around the waterfalls and started up it instead of following Crazy Runner. Crazy Runner yelled, "No, climb the rocks." Sam immediately started climbing the rocks after him.

The wolves were rapidly gaining on them. The rocks were too steep and slick for the wolves to climb. Crazy Runner pulled out his bow and killed another wolf.

This time the wolves did something that Crazy Runner had never seen wolves do before. They split into two groups. One group of about six wolves went downstream just out of arrow range. The white wolf led the rest up the trail about the waterfalls so they would be waiting when Crazy Runner and Sam reached the top.

Crazy Runner found a ledge wide enough for both of them to sit and talk. Sam asked, "Why did the white one take off up that trail?"

"That trail is how the Indians get around the waterfalls. They will canoe up the river and then carry their canoe up the trail to above the waterfalls and continue to canoe up the river. That wolf is the smartest wolf I have ever heard of. If we climb up, they will be waiting for us. If we climb down the other group will be waiting. I had a run-in with that wolf last year. I was able to escape by going over to the other side of the river just above the waterfalls.

The only way I see for us to get out of here is swimming and I am not a good swimmer."

"Yous have saved me up til now, so's it my turn to saves you. I's good at swimmin'. Lets us work our way along this ledge to wheres we is directly above the water. Then you jumps as far out into the water as you can, I's will jump just after ya and grab you and pull you ta the other shore. Jest member to takes a deep breath on the way down an kicks you feets as soon as you hit the water."

Just like the last time, Crazy Runner secured everything he

was carrying as best as he could in his pack. Before he had time to think about it, he jumped. He put everything he had into it and was able to land in the water just about halfway across the river. As soon as he hit the water, he started kicking for all he was worth.

He was still underwater when he felt a big hand grab the back of his buckskins and pull him to the surface. Then he heard, "Don't fight me, just kicks yor feet."

The water was very cold. When Sam pulled Crazy Runner to his feet, they were just a couple of feet from the east shore. They both crawled up to shore and looked at the white wolf and the large pack on the opposite shore. At that moment, it started raining very hard. There was a little ice mixed in with the rain.

Crazy Runner knew that unless they got warm quickly they could be in real trouble. Crazy Runner knew exactly where they were. They had come out of the river just below where he had first met Big Jim. He grabbed Sam and they headed up the ridge. They found a little cave and quickly built a fire. The cave was so small that the rocks surrounding them quickly warmed up and helped not only to warm them up but with the heat radiating from all directions it also helped to quickly dry off their clothes.

Crazy Runner went out and killed a rabbit for them to eat. They had a little deer meat left, but this would provide a change of pace. Because ice was forming, they spent the night in the cave.

CHAPTER 38—OHIO

The next morning ice covered everything. Sam had not seen ice before. Crazy Runner decided to do the same thing that Big Jim had done with him, not say anything until after he slipped and fell.

Sure enough just a few steps out of the cave, Big Jim went down hard and fast. Crazy Runner laughed and then explained to Sam about ice and how to walk on it.

They started out north along the ridge. As they were walking along Crazy Runner remarked that there was a canoe hidden down below them and if they had a canoe, it would make the rest of the trip easier and faster.

Crazy Runner led him down to the shore and to the place where the canoe was hidden. The canoe had two large holes in it. Evidently, the Creek had found the canoe and put the holes in it. Sam inspected the canoe and said, "I am very good at fixing wooden things. It will take several hours, but I can fix it. I will need your tomahawk and knife. While I am doing this, I need you to go and find some limbs which we can use for oars after I work on them a little."

Crazy Runner said, "Let's haul it up the hill so you are well hidden from the river in case any Indians come floating down the river."

After doing that, Crazy Runner took off to find the appropriate limbs. He found one quickly but it took him over an hour to find a second one. When he got back he found that Sam already had one hole patched and was almost finished with the second hole.

"How did you do that?"

Sam replied, "The bark off Birch trees is very good for this purpose. Then I had to get some sap from a maple tree to act as glue. I heated the bark to make it pliable. Then I heated the sap to make it sticky and applied it to the bark and the existing part of the canoe around the hole. I then repeated the process on the inside. In cold weather like this it should set in about an hour. It will not withstand any sharp objects, but it should keep the water out."

It was not long before Sam had finished the holes. Then he took the tomahawk and quickly formed the two limbs into two oars.

"Where did you learn to work with wood like that?"

"On the plantation. There is always things to be done with wood."

By the time Sam had finished with the oars, he tested the two repairs to the canoe and pronounced them ready. They put all of Crazy Runner's gear in it, pushed it out into the water and let it set there for a few minutes. No water came in around the patches.

Both of them climbed in, making sure to stay clear of the patches and started paddling. Crazy Runner was in the rear so he could steer. He kept the canoe close enough to the shore so that if water did start coming in, all they had to do was to climb out and they should be able to stand up.

After about a half hour of paddling it was clear that the repairs were working and Crazy Runner steered them towards the middle of the river. Sam was very strong, much stronger than Crazy Runner. While he had never paddled a canoe before it only took him a few strokes and he had caught on. The canoe was moving much faster than Crazy Runner had anticipated, because of Sam's strength.

It was colder on the water, but the rowing motion was keeping them good and warm. Since their legs were motionless, they had them covered. Shortly after sundown, they came to the Ohio River. Crazy Runner had figured it would take them well into tomorrow before they reached it, but Sam was rowing so hard they moved upstream faster than Crazy Runner had gone downstream on the rafts.

Sam wanted to cross the river immediately. Crazy Runner said no. They would land, eat something and then rest for a while. Crazy Runner knew that it would not be good for a slave to be seen in this territory. That meant they would have to cross the river at night. They had been rowing very hard for about seven hours against the current. From his experience, Crazy Runner knew the currents in the Ohio were much stronger than what they had previously experienced.

They rested for about two hours. Then they put the canoe on their shoulders and started walking upriver. Sam did not understand why they were doing this when they could paddle, but he trusted Crazy Runner so he did it without saying anything.

After about two hours of walking, they came to a good place to put the canoe in the river. Crazy Runner explained that the

"Sit and be patient. When the attack comes, you just watch around the wall and take the place of someone who has been killed or wounded."

That seemed to make sense, but Crazy Runner felt like he should do something. He helped some of the women fetch water. He helped filling up powder horns. Then he decided that perhaps he should get some rest also. He found a place and lay down.

He did not have time to get to sleep before both of the lookouts came running back. It was now late afternoon. Both men said they each saw the Indians and they were definitely painted for war. They felt the Indians were about one hour away. Crazy Runner went up to the wall and used his telescope to look to the east. A little over 30 minutes later, he was able to see the Indians approaching. Two other men with telescopes had spotted them at the same time.

Crazy Runner then saw small bands of Seneca taking off in different directions. About an hour later, everyone in the fort could see the smoke from the burning homes. Some of the children became frightened and started crying and their mothers were trying their best to calm them.

Shortly before dark, two men in military uniforms marched up to the fort carrying a white flag. Crazy Runner took a bead on one of the men and the man next to him said, "Don't shoot. That there flag means he wants to talk, peaceable like."

The front gate was opened slightly and the two men marched in. The gate closed after them. The two men marched to almost the center of the fort and stopped. One of them said, "Who is in charge here?" in English with a heavy French accent.

A man stepped forward and said, "My name is Hackett. Speak your piece."

"Mr. Hackett, all of your homes have been burned. You no

One of the women started yelling out things for the women and children to do. Crazy Runner noticed that everyone was remaining calm and no one was panicking.

Crazy Runner said to a man standing next to him, "You people been through this type of thing before?"

"Yep," as he spit some tobacco juice, "We been here a little over a year and this be the fourth injun attack. It is unusual for them to attack in cold weather like this. Mighty lucky for us you seen them or else we would not have been ready for them."

Crazy Runner thought that might be the reason why the Indians had chosen this time to attack; they figured the settlers would not be alert.

The women were working gathering water and making sandwiches for the men. They also set up in the store to be ready to reload rifles and pistols. The men were helping others to get to the fort and setting up positions around the walls of the fort. It looked like each man already had his assigned position and each man was setting up things the way he liked them at his place.

By noon every man, woman, and child within a couple of miles in every direction was inside the fort. As soon as each man had his place around the wall set up a guard schedule was established. Starting in the early afternoon the men started taking naps in any comfortable warm place they could find.

Crazy Runner asked one man, "The Seneca are about to attack. Why are the men taking naps?"

The man answered, "The Seneca are not that superstitious about attacking at night like the Shawnee and Creek. By getting some rest now, they will be more alert whenever the attack does come. We sent two men out in slightly different directions to give us advanced warning when they see them."

"What do you want me to do?" asked Crazy Runner.

current was so strong that all they were going to try to do was to get across the river. The current would probably take them downstream quite aways as they were paddling across. If they were lucky they would not go any further downstream than where they had first come to the Ohio River. Once on the Ohio side, they would start looking for the right plantation.

Crazy Runner had been correct. As they headed directly across the river, the current was carrying them downriver. However, Sam was so eager to see his wife and children again; he was paddling even stronger than he had before. Crazy Runner, trying as hard as he could, was not able to keep up with all of the strokes Sam was using. They got across and had only gone downstream about half of the distance Crazy Runner had thought they would.

When they climbed out of the water on the Ohio side, Sam wanted to start running, because he was now so close to his wife and children. Crazy Runner told him that this was Shawnee or Seneca territory, both wanted scalps and he would be no good to his family dead.

This made sense to Sam so he followed Crazy Runner's advice.

They carried the canoe upstream along the river for about two hours. They found a large cave. They could put the canoe there, build a fire and get some much needed sleep.

Crazy Runner had no trouble sleeping. Sam could not sleep because that river he could hear was the Ohio River and he knew that meant he was now close to his wife and four children

Chapter 39—Finding the Plantation

When they awoke, the ground was covered with a light dusting of snow. Crazy Runner said, "We have to stay right here in this cave for a while."

Sam angrily said, "Why, when we is so close?"

"Because it is more important for you to see your wife and children than it is to die when you are this close just because you are careless. That snow will make it very easy for Indians to see we are here and to track us. If we wait a few hours the snow should be melted and then we can go."

Sam did not say anything, but he sat down.

Crazy Runner continued, "You never did tell me what you are going to do once you find your wife and children. Are you going to become a slave for this man or are you going to steal them away? If you steal them away, where are you going to go? How are you going to make a living to feed your family?"

From the look on Sam's face it appeared that he had not considered any of these things. After giving it some thought, Sam replied, "I always knows I don't want to be a slave anymore. I always knows I don't want my wife and children to be slaves. I can make a good living with my hands and working with wood, but I don't know where I can do that."

They continued to talk for a while and Sam became more relaxed. Every now and then Crazy Runner would check outside. About noon all of the snow had melted.

Crazy Runner said, "We can leave now. We are going to leave the canoe in this cave for safety. We are going to go inland until we can barely see the river and follow it upriver until we come to the Allegheny. Once we find that we will search on this side of the Allegheny and if we don't find them we will cross over to the other side and look."

"Thank you. But why are you being so good to me?"

"As I already told you we have a lot in common, about the ship, losing our parents on the trip over and being raised in slavery. I ran away from it and you ran away from it. I don't have a family and I don't really want to settle down. You do have a family and I envy you that, so I am going to help you find your family and help you get them away from the plantation. After that, I am not yet sure what will happen."

"Thank you."

They left the cave and headed northeast. The ground was not snow covered except in a few places and they avoided them. Sam was careful to walk in Crazy Runner's footprints. Whenever they came to an open space to be crossed, they would run full speed.

In the late afternoon, they saw smoke ahead of them. They circled to the north to go around. When they got to a high place, Crazy Runner used his telescope to check out the smoke. It had been a cabin, but was now burning. Crazy Runner gave the telescope to Sam to see.

After he looked Sam gave Crazy Runner a surprised look. Crazy Runner whispered, "That is why we must be careful!"

They found a good dry spot out of the wind to spend the night.

The next morning they continued following the river only a little more inland than the previous day. They only saw the river occasionally.

About an hour before sunset, they came to a rise and saw the Allegheny River. They also saw two plantations on this side of the Allegheny, one was right on the interection of the rivers and across the river from the camp where Crazy Runner had gotten his telescope and tomahawk and the other was north and upstream several miles. From this vantage point, it was easy to see which was the main house and which were the slave quarters for both of them.

They walked toward the first one. Sam wanted to run, but Crazy Runner told him they had to get there a couple of hours after sunset when people were asleep. This made sense to Sam, so he walked.

When they got to the first one, they carefully snuck up to the slave quarters. Crazy Runner stood guard outside while Sam slipped inside. About five minutes later Sam came out alone. He went over to Crazy Runner and said, "They ain't here. These slaves want to run away with us."

"You have to make a choice, your family or them. All of us together would be too easy to track."

Sam shook his head and they headed north. The night was moon bright and there was a nice road so they ran. It did not take long to get to the second plantation.

Once again, Crazy Runner stood guard and Sam went into the slave quarters. About a minute after Sam entered the door Crazy Runner heard a scream that was very short. About five minutes passed and Sam and his family came out of the cabin and over to Crazy Runner.

Sam started to make introductions and Crazy Runner motioned for everyone to be quiet. They followed him up into the hills to the west. They walked the rest of the night and all of the next day. During the walk, Sam introduced Crazy Runner to his wife, Mabel and their children. They stopped only for water and to eat berries, what little deer meat they had left was gone by noon.

In the middle of the night, they arrived back at the cave where the canoe was hidden. Crazy Runner told the woman and children to stay there and for Sam to come with him.

They didn't have to travel far before Crazy Runner spotted a deer and killed it with an arrow. He told Sam to take it back to the cave, skin it and cook it. He was going to go kill another.

An hour after Sam had arrived back at the cave Crazy Runner came in carrying a big buck with large antlers. Crazy Runner told Sam to skin the second deer and cook all of that meat for their trip. Crazy Runner told Sam to make moccasins for his family out of one deerskin and a blanket out of the other as soon as they were dried. He was to take the antlers and make knives out of them.

Then Crazy Runner explained he was going to backtrack and cover their trail. Then he was going to the settlement across the Allegheny to get some information. Sam was to stay here in the cave, do those things and wait until Crazy Runner returned.

CHAPTER 40—SUPPLIES

Crazy Runner backtracked about five miles covering all of the tracks as he went. Then he made a false trail heading due north about two miles and had it disappear in some rocks. He then backtracked and carefully headed east leaving no trail. When he got to a high place, he saw a group of three men following the trail all of them had followed. He watched as the men came to the place where he had made the false trail and the men followed it without even slowing down.

As he continued east, he was very proud of himself. Big Jim had shown him how to leave a false trail and those men had not even hesitated.

He reached the Allegheny River just before dark and he started downstream. It was too cold for him to grab on to a log and try to float across. He came to a cabin with a canoe outside. Crazy Runner went to the cabin and asked the man if he would give him a ride to the other side. The man said, "No, but just a little ways downstream is a raft someone just left there, you can pole your way across."

CRAZY RUNNER - TRAILBLAZER - 1750

It did not take long to find the raft and a limb he could use for a pole. He was able to get across without trouble. He landed the raft just above the settlement and pulled the raft up into some brush.

He walked into the settlement and just walked around. It was good to be around a large group of people again. He went to the place Big Jim had gone to when he left Crazy Runner for the night with the settlers. There were many men there and several women who were dressed only in their undergarments. While almost everyone knew Big Jim, no one had seen him in some time.

He found a warm place to sleep and settled down for the night.

The next morning he was wandering around the trading area when he heard someone shout his name. He looked around and saw Hank Jacobs.

As they shook hands, Hank said, "I am sure glad I found you. I have a big problem. We came up here to trade pelts for supplies for our settlement. There were five of us when we started out, but two got killed when we had a run in with some Creek just above the waterfalls. The rest of us got here with most of the pelts, but just three of us can't get all of the supplies we need back town to the settlement. We have one very large raft, we need four to pole and one to steer. Can you help us and find one other person? We have asked just about everyone we can find around here and all of the people here now are trappers and not interested in settling down. They say the settler folks won't be arriving here for another month and we don't want to wait that long."

Crazy Runner said, "I know a family, father, mother, two young sons and two young daughters, who are looking for a place to settle. He is very good at making things out of wood.

She is a hard worker. They have no supplies or money, but they are willing to work hard."

"That sounds wonderful. We would stake them in exchange for their help in getting the supplies back to the settlement." Hank said happily.

"Hank, they are a family of escaped Negro slaves."

There was a moment of silence as the three men looked at each other and then Hank said, "We have two very friendly families of Cherokee living and farming in the valley now, if you are willing to vouch for these folks, then why not."

"I have no money, but I could use a couple of powder horns and a good knife, will you stake me?"

"Pick out what you want and I will pay for it. How soon can you leave?"

"As soon as I can pick them up. Have you seen Big Jim here?"

"I haven't seen him since he left with you." Hank said.

Less than an hour later, they were at the water's edge with the raft.

Crazy Runner instructed them to stay along the north shore of the Ohio until he told them to stop. Shortly before dark, he told them to stop and make a camp with no fire. "I will be back before morning with the family."

When Crazy Runner reached the cave, Sam had put the deerskins in a position outside between two trees in a high wind area so they had dried quickly and had already made moccasins for the family. All of the meat had been cooked and they were ready to travel.

Crazy Runner said, "I have three men upriver. They have a large raft with supplies on them that they are taking to their settlement. On the way up here two of them were killed by Indians. If you and your wife are willing to help them get those supplies to their settlement, they want you to settle there and they will give you some supplies to get you started. To show you their good faith, here is your own knife, so you can now give me back mine."

Mabel quickly ran up to Crazy Runner and hugged him. Crazy Runner got very embarrassed. Sam laughed and said, "Let's go meet our new neighbors. What do we do about the canoe?"

"Leave it here. I will use it."

It took the entire family about twice the amount of time to get to Hank Jacobs camp as it had taken Crazy Runner to get to the cave. By the time the introductions were finished the sun was beginning to come up.

Hank Jacobs explained to each person what their job would be on the trip down the river. They said goodbye to Crazy Runner, boarded the rafts, and were on their way crossing the Ohio and heading home.

Chapter 41—Wounded

Crazy Runner watched them heading across the Ohio River as he was walking towards the cave. They poled until it was too deep and then they started paddling. Sam was on the downriver side and he was paddling so strong and fast that they were crossing more than going down river. They reached the opposite side a good mile above the river to the settlement.

Crazy Runner was proud of himself. Sam was a good man and Hank Jacobs and the others in the settlement were good people. He was sure they would get along just fine. He was a little surprised that two families of Cherokee had moved into the valley and wondered why; normally the Cherokee stay in their villages. Perhaps they were like the white man and simply looking for better farmland.

Crazy Runner reached the cave about the same time the raft turned into the river heading toward the settlement. Those on the raft waved to him and he waved back as they were disappearing from view.

On the walk back to the cave, he had been thinking about

where to go now. Since he had been unable to find Big Jim at the trading post, which was part of the reason he had guided Sam to Ohio, he was not sure exactly what he wanted to do. He went into the cave and saw that they had left quite a bit of cooked deer meat in the canoe. It was enough to keep him full for a week.

He knew he did not want to walk around this side of the Ohio River for two reasons: he had seen what the Seneca had done to white men and if he were to go further north, it would be even colder than it was here. He decided to float down the Ohio River for a while.

He got the canoe out of the cave and carefully carried it to the water's edge. There was a small inlet and he put the canoe in the water there. The patches were still holding. He put in his gear and then he got in and just sat there for a minute to make sure the patches held. Then he went out of the inlet and started down river staying on the north side, while eating a nice piece of deer meat.

He had traveled about a mile past the mouth of the river where the raft had gone when he saw an Indian village on this side of the river. He was not sure what tribe it was, but he immediately started paddling across the river. When he got out into the river he could tell that it was a Seneca village. He heard a yell and started paddling even harder and faster trying to get as much distance between him and the camp as quickly as possible. He would have felt much better if his feet were on the ground and he was running.

Arrows started flying in his direction. He was a little over half-way across the river when one arrow hit him in his right thigh. He remembered what Big Jim had said about an arrow wound; do not pull it out until you are ready to doctor it. It hurt a lot but he could not stop paddling. He was about ¾ of the way across when two arrows barely missed him, one went through the floor of the boat just in front of him and the other went through the floor just behind him. Water started pouring in.

He waited until the canoe was about 1/3 full of water and he jumped out, grabbing his gear. Luckily, he found that he was standing only about waist deep in the water. He made his way to shore and into the brush. As he was going into the brush, he looked over his shoulder and saw that they were not pursuing him.

He had to get somewhere he could make a fire quickly. He found a gully with a lot of dry wood and it had trees fully covering it. He quickly started a fire. As the fire got started, he looked at the arrow. It was not deep, but it was bleeding a lot. He put his knife in the fire to heat it up. As soon as it was hot, he took this tomahawk and put the handle in his mouth to chomp on. Then in one motion, he pulled the arrow out with his left hand while he touched the heated knife to his skin, just as Big Jim had told him. It burned the skin to stop the bleeding and caused a great deal of pain. He screamed and passed out.

When he came to, he was not sure how long he had been unconscious, but the fire was almost out. He examined his leg and saw that it was no longer bleeding, although it did throb with a great deal of pain. He was glad he had something to eat earlier. Big Jim had told him whenever you lose blood you need to not move much for one day and drink a lot of water.

That meant he had to find water. He could hear the river, but he knew it would not be safe to go in that direction. He also knew that the river had many little streams coming off in this direction. He concentrated to remember the shoreline as he was paddling toward it. He remembered what looked like a small stream that he had been trying to head for, but the current and sinking boat had not allowed him to reach it. That meant it would be east of here.

Using his rifle as a crutch, he slowly started walking east. He had only gone about 50 feet when he found it. A short distance away was a lot of brush where he could lay down and rest. He drank as much as he could and crawled into the brush and went to sleep.

He was startled awake by a sound. From where he was, he could not tell exactly what was making the sound, but he could tell that there was more than one of them. He knew he could not run and he was not strong enough to fight whatever it was, so his best course of action was to remain hidden and hoped it was not wolves. Since he had entered the water to get to these bushes he was certain that no man or animal would be able to track him to his hiding place as long as he did not make a sound.

Whoever or whatever it was, they were not attempting to be silent. He then heard voices and they were in the direction of his fire. Now he figured it was the Indians from across the river. When he had gotten out of the water, they had seen he was wounded, so they must have figured he would be an easy kill and had come after him. They followed his trail to the stream.

There were three of them and they were Seneca. Very carefully and slowly he got his pistol and tomahawk out and put them on the ground in front of him. Then he remembered the water. He had been waist deep in the river so the powder in the pistol was probably wet. His rifle had been under the water in the canoe so the powder was definitely wet. His two powder horns had been hanging around his neck and that powder was dry, but it would be noisy to reloading either the pistol or rifle. That meant that his tomahawk and knife were his only weapons.

They found where he had entered the stream. They looked puzzled. One of them searched on the opposite side, one went upstream, and the third went downstream. The one who crossed the stream came within five feet of Crazy Runner. About ten minutes later, the one who had gone upstream started yelling. The other two quickly went running in that direction.

Crazy Runner waited about 30 minutes and then slowly crawled out, got a good drink of water and went back to his hiding place. He opened up his powder horns. The two that were around his neck were dry. The one in his pack was wet. He took powder from one of the dry powder horns and loaded the rifle and pistol. He then took off the quiver of arrows, removed the arrows and spread the quiver out on the ground. He poured the wet powder on to it. Then he lay down and went back to sleep.

When he awoke, it was full dark. He listened very carefully for some time. He ate some deer meat as he listened. Since he had heard nothing, when he had finished eating he went to the stream and got a very big drink, put the powder back into the powder horn, grabbed his gear, and started walking southwest.

His right leg was stiff, but it no longer throbbed with pain. He stopped every now and then to check and make sure it was not bleeding. After about an hour of walking, the leg was no longer stiff. Every time he came to water, he drank and drank a lot. He also ate more deer meat, more than he usually did.

By the time the sun came up, he was feeling in good spirits. He tried running a short distance and felt the skin tighten where it had been burned, but there was no real pain. He had survived his first wound, thanks to Big Jim teaching him what to do.

There was still a lot of territory on the southern side of the Ohio that he decided to check out. If he went to the same village of Shawnee, he knew he would be accepted because he had run their gauntlet.

Chapter 42—Safety

He walked west, about 100 yards south of the Ohio River, but still parallel to it. Whenever possible he would climb to a high place and observe. At the first location, he looked across the Ohio and could see the Seneca village. Looking down the river, he saw another Indian village across the river. Since it was just a few miles from the first village, he reasoned they must be Seneca also.

Near the end of the day, he came to one high place and almost as soon as he reached it, he could hear a commotion not far away. There was a group of Shawnee braves on this side of the river and a group of Seneca on the other side. Both were shouting insults to the other. He did not understand everything, but understood enough to know that one of the insults the Shawnee were shouting was calling the Seneca some type of dog.

He went further inland and then continued in the same direction as the river until he found a place to make camp. With the Shawnee riled up over the Seneca, he figured he should not make a fire. He woke up in the middle of the night shivering and sweating at the same time. He did not understand this. He knew he had to find shelter. He got up, gathered his belongings, and started walking west.

He had walked about four hours when he realized he had no idea where he was. He was just wandering around aimlessly. He came upon a stream and got a drink. As he was getting up, he collapsed and passed out.

Two days later, he awoke. He was wrapped in furs, in a Shawnee sweat lodge, with a medicine man chanting and an old woman washing off his face. As soon as she realized he was conscious, the woman started feeding him some broth. It tasted good. He kept drifting off to sleep and whenever he would come to the woman would again feed him some broth. This process kept repeating for two more days.

On the fifth day, he awoke feeling very hungry. He saw his pack on the other side of the tent and started to go for it, when he realized he was naked. He quickly pulled the furs back over himself and the woman smiled, handed him his clothes and left. His clothes had been washed and the hole in his pants from the arrow had been mended. He dressed, went to his pack, got the largest piece of deer meat, and started eating. When he had finished that, he got a smaller piece of deer meat and started eating that as he walked out of the sweat lodge.

The woman had picked up his things and motioned for him to follow her as she went to another lodge and placed his things inside. When he looked inside, he saw Black Wolf.

Crazy Runner smiled and said, "How did I get to your village?"

"Some scouts found you, recognized you, and brought you back here." Then Black Wolf asked, "Who shot you?"

"Seneca."

"Where?"

"When I was canoeing down the Ohio River."

"Why were you going down the river? I thought you liked to run?" and he laughed. "You did a good job of patching up your wound. Where did you learn that?"

"After I left here I met a trapper named Big Jim. I traveled with him for a while and he taught me many things."

"I know this Big Jim. He is a good man. What you do now?"

"Since I no longer have a canoe, now I will do more running." They both laughed. "I was thinking about following the Ohio River and see what is along it. Then I will go through Creek country and let them chase me." They both laughed.

Black Wolf said, "Be careful. There are bad white men down river. The Creek are on the warpath against Shawnee and white men."

"Yes, I know. I saw a white man's village they had wiped out. They had a Frenchman with them and Big Jim killed him. I saw a Frenchman with the Creek when they attacked this village."

"Both the English and French say they want the Shawnee to be their friends and attack settlers. The French send the Seneca and the Creek against us and the English send the Oneida and Tuscarora against us. Our chiefs have been discussing this situation for many moons."

"If the Shawnee go with one side or the other, will I still be welcome in the Shawnee camp?"

"Always, because you have proven your bravery to the Shawnee by running the gauntlet."

Chapter 43—Thieves

The following morning he said goodbye to Black Wolf and headed off to the west. Not wanting to disappoint the Shawnee, he ran until he was well out of sight. He remembered that Black Wolf had warned him about the Creek and bad white men. He began wondering if when he said bad white men he had meant the French or the English or both.

It appeared to him that it was warming up. He could not see his breath in the early morning and he started sweating a little around the middle of the day. He took off his coat, stuffed it in his pack, and continued on his way.

At one high point, he observed three rafts on the Ohio River at the same time. Two were poling their way up river and one was going down river. The ones going up river seemed to be telling the ones going down river about something, perhaps a warning.

This got Crazy Runner curious. He decided to travel a little closer to the river. It was warmer and there were some open areas, so he decided to run. He ran all the way to the river's edge, which was about five miles from where he had started on top of a high ridge. All of the rafts were out of sight when he got there.

He went back into cover and continued down river. In the early afternoon, he came to place where he could look down on an inlet off the river. It was only about 100 yards from the river to the end of the inlet, but at the end of the inlet was an open area with several large tents set up. He could see several men and women around the area. He also noticed some men at the entrance to the inlet.

Crazy Runner thought the tents looked like a temporary trading post. There appeared to be no customers now. Crazy Runner started down to the tents. When he was about 75 yards away and still under the cover of the brush and trees, he hid his pack in some brush, which was a trick Big Jim had taught him. Sometimes the traders would give you a better price or something free if they thought you were down on your luck.

As he walked into the camp, all he had was his rifle, knife, bow and arrows and the clothes on his back. He stopped at the edge of the inlet and took a drink of water. There was something wrong with the water it had a foul taste. He had never tasted anything like that before.

Two men were walking up to him just as there was a shot coming from where the inlet joined to the river. Immediately, the two men stopped in their tracks. They looked back at the tent and an older man signaled for them to come back.

Crazy Runner just stood there observing. Three rafts entered the inlet, each one with two men on it. All three rafts were piled high with furs. As the rafts reached the end of the inlet, Crazy Runner also started in that direction. He figured that he would not stand out so much in the crowd.

Crazy Runner went into the largest tent where many things

were for sale. The people who ran this place were paying a lot of attention to the men from the rafts and not paying much attention to Crazy Runner. Crazy Runner went around each table looking at the merchandise. One thing caught his eye; it was a telescope with a "BJ" scratched in it. Crazy Runner picked it up and started examining it. One of the men there hollered, "Boy, don't be handling the merchandise unless you have some money."

Crazy Runner put it down, thinking that perhaps Big Jim had traded it for some liquor or one of the women in the small tents. When he went over to where the weapons were he saw Big Jim's rifle and pistol, he knew them because of the "BJ" carved in them.

Crazy Runner said in a loud voice, "This rifle and pistol and that there telescope all belong to Big Jim. I have traveled with him and I know he would never sell them, so how did you get them?"

Immediately, the six men from the rafts started backing off with their rifles ready. Crazy Runner cocked his.

"Wait a minute fellas. I don't know who this Big Jim is, but an injun came in here a few days ago and sold them things to me for some likker."

One of the men off the raft said, "I know you, you are Crazy Runner. I'm Ben Jackson, you and Big Jim rode with us when we were taking in our last load of skins."

"I remember."

A rifle suddenly started pointing out of one of the tents towards Ben Jackson and Crazy Runner fired. A man fell out of the tent dead.

Crazy Runner said, as he was reloading, "Ben, he was going to shoot you."

Out of the woods on the west side of the inlet came several

shots. One of the raft men fell. Ben and two of his men immediately shot the three men in the tent. Everyone started taking cover.

As soon as his rifle was loaded, Crazy Runner whispered to Ben that he was going around behind the men in the woods. Crazy Runner ran full speed into the woods and up the hill. He kept running after he was in cover and then circled above the men who were shooting from the woods.

He got above them and saw that there were five of them. He shot the one who was closest to him with an arrow. Then he moved and shot another with an arrow. He was picking off the ones in the back first, just as Big Jim had taught him. He then shot at a third, but the man quickly stood just as Crazy Runner had let the arrow go and the arrow caught the man in the leg instead of the back. The man hollered and then the two remaining men took off running.

Crazy Runner yelled to Ben that the men were running away. He also yelled at the wounded one to get out into the clearing. He did and Crazy Runner went down the hill.

Ben was already bandaging up his wounded man. Crazy Runner led the man he had wounded over to the big tent. The man sat down and Crazy Runner said, "How did you get Big Jim's things?"

The man said, "An injun sold em."

Then Crazy Runner grabbed the arrow, pushed it in a little farther and moved it around with the man screaming in agony. Then he said one more time, "How did you get Big Jim's things?"

"All right, he was already camped here when we arrived. He had a nice stack of furs so the old man, who you already kilt, shot him and he fell in the river."

"When was this?"

"About four day ago."

Then Crazy Runner took his knife, stuck it in the man's stomach, and twisted it as he pulled it out. He then turned and walked away with the man falling to the ground and screaming in agony. Ben said, "Big Jim taught you that."

Crazy Runner nodded.

Ben said, "What we do now is take what we want, then burn this place and everything in it."

Crazy Runner asked, "What about the women?"

"They no better than this trash. We won't kill em, but we will leave them here on their own."

Crazy Runner grabbed Big Jim's rifle, pistol, and telescope. With some looking he also found on of Big Jim's powder horns, but could not find his tomahawk or knife. He grabbed some shot, wadding, flints and jerky.

Ben found several kegs of powder, they put one full keg on a raft, and they each filled their powder horns from another. They spread some powder around and set fire to it running like crazy to their rafts. When the other powder kegs exploded, it caught the big tent on fire and the four women came running out of the tents. All of the women were only dressed in their underwear. Crazy Runner started towards where he had hidden his things.

Ben hollered to Crazy Runner, "You're mighty welcome to travel with us."

"Thanks, but I already been in that direction."

He put Big Jim's pistol in his belt; he put Big Jim's telescope and other things in his pack, and then headed on his way west, following the river. He looked like he was ready for a fight, with two pistols in his belt and a rifle in each hand.

CHAPTER 44—CARELESS

Crazy Runner decided to head down river. He was hoping that when Big Jim fell in the river he had just been wounded and he might be laid up along the shore west of here. He traveled the rest of the day without a sign of anyone coming out of the water.

At sundown, the moon was out bright. He kept going looking for any signs. A couple of hours later he realized how tired he was and made camp. He lay down but could not get to sleep. As he lay there, he recalled everything that had happened that day. He realized that he did not feel sorry for killing those men, because those men probably would have killed him. They were probably what Black Wolf was talking about when he said, "Bad white men". Then he started thinking about all of the traveling he had done with Big Jim and all of the things Big Jim had taught him. Finally, he fell asleep.

The sun shining on his face woke him up. It was the dawn of a new day. The sun was out bright. He gathered up everything and decided to take off running. He had not run far, when he realized that the pack was not resting well and was beating him as he ran. He stopped and used two of the straps in his belt to hold up dear to tie the bottom of the pack around his waist. When he started running again he found that had done the trick, the pack no longer swung out and then came down hitting him on the back.

He continued down river for another day. He noticed two Indian villages on the other side of the river, but did not come across any on this side. He did not find any sign of anyone leaving the river. He would have to live with the fact that Big Jim was dead. When he finally realized that, he felt as though there was a large empty hole inside him.

The next day Crazy Runner started inland. He was still thinking a lot about Big Jim and not paying attention to his surroundings. Suddenly, he was brought back to reality as an arrow flew by him and hit a tree a few inches away. He quickly took off running looking in all directions as he ran. He had failed to realize that he was no longer in Shawnee territory but in Creek territory.

If he had been paying attention there had been signs of many Indians for the last hour, but in his grief, he had not noticed them. These Creek were painted for war and must have been headed to attack the Shawnee.

Quickly, gathering his senses, the Creek were east of him and the Shawnee were northeast of this location. Therefore, he took off southwest. Crazy Runner thought that the Creek would not be as likely to follow him very far if he were headed in the opposite direction from where they were headed.

He could not tell exactly, but about ten braves started after him. There was a loud sound, it was similar to a sound some Cherokee make when blowing through an empty powder horn, and after that only two of Creek continued after him. It took him about three hours of running at full speed before the two Creek stopped chasing him. Not wanting to take any chances, Crazy Runner turned south and continued running full speed for another hour.

The Creek were tricky. Big Jim had taught him that sometimes a few Creek would follow directly after someone, while others went on parallel trails out of sight. Then the braves following directly behind would stop and hide, making the one being followed think they had given up the attack when the two groups on either side were still going.

He came to a rocky hill, climbed up in among the rocks and readied his two rifles as he waited. With no sign of the Creek in two hours, he was satisfied that they were no longer after him; perhaps the loud noise was to call the warriors back. He was also mad at himself for not paying attention to his surroundings. He knew that in this country a man has to forget yesterday and think only of today; yet in his grief he had forgotten that so very important point. He had to make sure that would never happen again, his life relied on it.

Slowly and carefully, trying always to remain hidden, Crazy Runner climbed up the rocky hill. When he got near the top, he found a secluded place back in some brush and used his telescope to survey all around him. He saw another war party of Creek east of him and they also were headed northeast.

He crawled over the ridge so his silhouette would not stand out. When he found another secluded area, he viewed this side of the ridge. He saw two villages that must be Creek villages.

He thought that with the two large war parties the only people left in those villages must be old men, women, and children. That should make it easier to travel around those villages.

He knew by the time he reached the bottom on this side it

would be close to dark. He went down about halfway and found a nice secluded place to spend the night.

Chapter 45—Young Hunter

The next day he continued down to the bottom of the hill and headed in a southeasterly direction so he would be traveling between the two villages. From the ridge, he had seen that the two villages were about three miles apart, with plenty of dense woods located between them.

He was purposefully concentrating on his surroundings, watching and listening very intently as he walked. This concentration allowed him not to think about Big Jim.

He was following an animal trail. He noticed that someone else was following this animal trail. By the size of the moccasins, he thought it was probably a boy. He continued following the animal trail while slowing his pace and being positive that he was very quiet.

He heard something in the trail ahead of him and quickly got off the trail and hid. A deer came down the trail full speed from the direction Crazy Runner was heading. An arrow landed about a foot from Crazy Runner. Crazy Runner slowly moved a few feet farther from the trail.

An Indian boy came running up the trail. He appeared to be only about eight or nine years old. He was not yet an experienced hunter. His shot had been about four feet behind and six feet to the right of the deer. He was not accurate and had the wrong angle.

The boy stopped and started looking for his arrow. Crazy Runner could see that the boy only had the one arrow. The boy was coming directly toward Crazy Runner although he was only looking down for his arrow. Crazy Runner took a stone and threw it where the arrow had landed. The boy quickly turned in that direction looking intently for what had made the sound when he saw his arrow.

The young rarely think about more than one thing at a time. Instead of wondering what had made the noise, the boy's attention when directly to the lost arrow. The boy picked up his arrow and shot it toward a tree that was about six feet away from him. He missed it.

Crazy Runner wanted to help him but knew that if he showed himself that the boy would run back to his village and alert the others. His chances were much better if no one knew where he was. Crazy Runner slowly crept a little further away just in case the boy started shooting in his direction again.

The boy kept trying to shoot at trees. It seemed like several hours. Crazy Runner was getting very thirsty. He could hear a stream, but the stream was back in the direction of the boy.

Finally, from about four feet away the boy was able to hit the tree and make the arrow stick. This was evidently good enough for him. He pulled his arrow out and headed in the direction from which he had come.

Crazy Runner waited a while and then slowly moved toward the stream. When he got there, he took a long drink. As he was drinking, he heard talking. It was Indian women. He could hear them, but could not see them.

Crazy Runner quietly crossed the stream. Just as he reached the other side, he could barely see some Indian women downstream washing clothes. He moved downstream a little and used his telescope to observe whether there were any braves with them. He could see six women washing clothes. One large woman was standing there holding a stick. It appeared as though she were hitting someone now and then. Bushes were blocking Crazy Runner from seeing who was being hit. He assumed it was a captive from another tribe.

After about ten minutes, the women all got up and started moving back toward the village. Crazy Runner was amazed that the woman being hit had light brown hair, very close to the color of his hair. This was a captive white woman. The large woman hit her again because she was not moving fast enough. The white woman picked up her pace.

Crazy Runner followed them at a distance. When they got to their village, he found a small ridge from where he could observe the entire village.

There were many teepees. As he was looking around the camp with his telescope, he saw some children playing. One was a little boy with blond hair. The little boy went up to the white woman and they hugged each other. The large Indian woman then hit the mother, the white woman went back to work and the boy went back to playing.

Crazy Runner counted 6 old men, 23 women, 18 children and a few babies in the village during the hour he observed. As soon as he had seen the white woman, he knew he must try to save her. He also knew that he could not do it during the daytime. It was only early afternoon so he had to wait all day. The braves were with the war party so it would be a little easier.

Slowly he circled the entire camp getting a view from every angle. He found a comfortable place to wait and observe.

CHAPTER 46—RESCUE

Several times during the afternoon, Crazy Runner had observed the white woman and the blond boy going in and out of one teepee. It was the only teepee that both of them had gone into. He had not seen anyone else going into that teepee.

It was an hour after sundown before everyone seemed to be in their teepees. He waited another hour and then slowly circled the camp to the point closest to the white woman's teepee. He hid his rifles, bow and arrows, pistols and pack. Then he started slowly into the camp, staying on his feet, but as low as possible.

He got to the back of woman's teepee and stopped, carefully looking and listening. He started to move around to the entrance of the teepee when an old man came out of the next teepee. Crazy Runner stopped and got out his tomahawk. The old man moved a few feet, dropped his pants and peed. Then he pulled up his pants and went back into his teepee.

Crazy Runner waited until he thought that the old man might be back to sleep. Then he crawled into the teepee. The woman was on one side of the teepee and the boy was sleeping on the other. Crazy Runner slowly moved over the woman and put his hand tight over the woman's mouth. She jerked awake and looked at him. Crazy Runner whispered, "I am going to take you out of here, if you want to leave." She nodded yes and as he removed his hand, she started silently crying.

"Wake up the boy and keep him quiet, we need to get moving now. No talking until I tell you."

She silently woke up her son and warned him to make no noise. They followed Crazy Runner out of the tent and back to where he had left his things. He loaded up and they started out. After they had traveled about an hour, they came to a stream. They went downstream in the water, with Crazy Runner carrying the boy and the woman carrying the two rifles. At one point a dead tree had fallen into the stream, they got on top of it and walked to the end. Then they walked on some rocks for a while. When they came to another stream, they went upstream until they came to another dead tree and left heading east.

Since there were no braves in the camp Crazy Runner felt there was no one in the village who could have trailed them this far. He found a good place to stop and they camped, but it would have to be a cold camp. The boy was asleep almost as soon as they stopped.

They sat down and Crazy Runner said, "I am Crazy Runner. Who are you and where did you come from?"

"My name is Danielle Bowerman and this is my son Caleb. We were with a group of settlers moving west when the Creek attacked us. My husband and all of the other men were killed and scalped. Those women and children who weren't killed were divided up and sent to different villages.

Our guide, Colin Owens, led us into a trap. The Indians were waiting for us. When the fighting was over I saw a French soldier pay Owens in gold."

Crazy Runner said, "Get a couple of hours of sleep and then we need to start moving again."

She lay down and rested, but her eyes remained intently watching Crazy Runner.

About two hours before sunrise Crazy Runner had her wake up her son. He gave them both some deer meat.

While they were eating, he asked her to describe this Colin Owens. Danielle answered, "He is a short man with brown hair, has a full grizzly beard and walks with a slight limp." Crazy Runner was sure that he had never seen anyone like that.

When they had finished he told them they needed to get started again. He knew that they would have to take many breaks. He wanted to travel a couple of more miles before daybreak.

Chapter 47—Traveling

Crazy Runner knew it would be a slow and hard journey. He was worried about the boy. He knew the boy would tire out easily, he was not sure if the boy could remain quiet when necessary, especially as active as he had observed him in the village. He also was not sure how much the woman had been through and exactly how strong she was.

In areas where he was certain it would be safe to talk they did. He found out the boy was seven years old. The woman was 26 and in good strong health. Her husband had been Edward Bowerman. They had been married for eight years before he was killed. They were originally from Prussia, but had sailed from England and had landed at Norfolk. From Norfolk, they had traveled to somewhere east of here where the ambush had taken place.

She said they had been traveling from Norfolk for almost a month when the ambush had taken place. She was not sure, but thought it had been about two months since the Creek had taken them captive. Crazy Runner thought it was odd for someone to lead a group west in wintertime.

"I had given up any hope of being rescued. I was about to be married to a brave when the men painted themselves, danced the war dance and left two days before you rescued me."

"That is what made it so easy for me to rescue you. The women sensed that you had given up and would not try to escape so they were not guarding you closely."

"Where are you taking us?"

"I know of a settlement of nice folks that would take you in. You will be safe there from the Indians. It is in Cherokee country and the Cherokee are friendly. That is about a week's walk. If you want to stay at that settlement that is fine, if you want to go back to Virginia, then someone from that settlement will probably be able to guide you. I have never been to Virginia."

"Where are you from?"

It took him about an hour to explain all about himself, but it took up the time while they were walking. He made sure that the talking was not distracting him from paying close attention to the surroundings.

The rest of the day Crazy Runner had noticed no signs of Indians. While the days had been getting noticeably warmer, the nights were still cold. That night he found a depression in which they could all fit around a nice fire. Because of the depression the fire could not been seen from a distance. The boy was good at getting good wood for the fire. Crazy Runner killed a couple of rabbits, so they ate well for supper. All three of them had a good night's sleep.

On the third day, Crazy Runner noticed many tracks. These tracks were not all Indians; there were many men with boots walking among them. This bothered Crazy Runner. That night, after the boy was asleep, Crazy Runner told Danielle about the bounty that the French and English had on settler's scalps and why they were doing that. He also told her that there were white military men traveling with the Indians whose trail they had crossed that day, so if she saw white men do not be eager to yell out and make sure to control the boy.

On the fourth day, they saw a large group of Creek from a distance. There were white men in French military uniforms with them. When Danielle looked through the telescope she told him, "Those men are French soldiers, just like you said."

Caleb liked looking through the telescope. Caleb took the telescope and looked around in every direction. When he looked back the way they had traveled he asked, "Are those Indians following us?"

Crazy Runner quickly took the telescope and looked where Caleb was pointing. He saw three braves and it did look like they were following their trail.

Crazy Runner immediately got everyone on their feet and moving. Before long, he found a good place for them to hide. He left the rifles, pistols, and his pack with them and he backtracked. He found a good place for his ambush.

He waited and waited and there was no sign of the three Indians. When he had seen them, they had been running. Crazy Runner figured that it would only take the Indians about fifteen to twenty minutes to overtake them and over an hour had passed.

He listened very carefully and heard nothing. Then we went over to a tree that was well guarded with brush and climbed it. The trees here were thick, but he could still see for a distance in several spots. Nothing was moving. He got out the telescope and looked. Nothing was moving. Evidently, the braves were not following their trail.

Then he remembered about the Creek following a parallel trail. He looked north and sure enough, there were the three braves. They were on a well-worn trail and moving fast. They were already past the point where he had hidden the woman and boy and were continuing east.

He thought they would continue east for a while and then turn south to wait in ambush. He ran back and got the woman and boy and they headed due north. Crazy Runner figured that those three would think that they had changed direction and probably head south to find the tracks since the general direction they had been traveling was southeast. When they got to the trail the Indians had taken they carefully crossed it, with Crazy Runner making sure they left no tracks.

They traveled until sundown and settled down. There was no safe place here to build a fire so it would be a cold camp.

The next day they traveled in an easterly direction, they did not want to run into the large group with the French soldiers, so they moved slowly. He was careful to stop every now and then to backtrack and cover their tracks. Late in the afternoon heavy clouds started coming in. He knew that in this part of the country the chance of finding a cave would be hard. He left Danielle and Caleb in a safe place and he ran in a large circle to find a safe place.

He found a high place with an overhang. They would be protected from the weather on three sides. The open side faced the west. The storm and wind was coming from the east, they should be safe.

He got Danielle and Caleb and moved them into the little safe area just as the rain started to fall. There was barely room for the three of them, but at least they were dry. He got his bearskin coat out of his pack and used it to cover the woman and boy. It rained hard the rest of the afternoon and all night. The next morning the rain slowly subsided as the morning progressed. By noon, it had stopped raining, but there were still many dark clouds. Crazy Runner ventured out to a location where he could look around.

He saw three small groups of Creeks. They were evidently scouting parties, as they were not wearing war paint. Crazy Runner went back and told Danielle that they would have to stay here until tomorrow. The ground was too wet and they would leave tracks that would make them easy to follow. They had plenty to eat. There was a well-covered rock trail to a stream for water. Crazy Runner also figured that the woman and boy needed a good rest. They had been traveling hard for five days. The sun came out in the afternoon, warmed things up and dried out the ground.

The next morning they continued heading east. The traveling was slow. They would cover in one hour the distance that Crazy Runner would usually cover in five minutes. Crazy Runner tried to pick routes that were easiest for the woman and boy; if it were up to him they would be traveling as close to the very top of the ridges as possible, but the going was much more strenuous there. During the last two days, Caleb seemed to be getting slower and slower. Today he was back up to speed.

At a high place in the afternoon Crazy Runner was finally able to see the Blue Mountains and the mountains that contained Hank Jacobs settlement. At the rate they were traveling, he thought they would probably reach the settlement in three more days, which was about three days longer than he had first calculated.

During this day, they saw signs of more Creek, but did not actually see any Indians and most of the signs were at least two days old. Crazy Runner thought that most of the Creek were probably north in a battle with the Shawnee or at least that is what he was hoping.

CHAPTER 48—MORE SETTLERS

They camped for the night. About an hour after dark, Crazy Runner went to a ridge to scout. They were still in Creek territory here so he thought they should not have a campfire. To the east, he saw a very large fire. It was too far away for him to see anything in detail, but with the telescope, he was able to make out several people moving around the fire. That camp was directly in line with where he wanted to go. He figured that traveling at the rate the three of them had been they would be about where that fire was by this time tomorrow. However, if that group were traveling west, then they would meet during the day tomorrow.

When they got moving the next morning, Crazy Runner was not planning to travel all day. He just wanted to go far enough to find a safe place at a higher elevation where Danielle and Caleb could settle while he scouted. It took nearly two hours, but he found a place that was at a high enough elevation where they could see in several directions for quite a distance, because the brush was so thick, they could not be seen.

Crazy Runner left them there and went scouting. He had only gone about a mile when he stopped and climbed a tall tree on the side of a hill. When he had gotten as far up as he could safely climb without being seen, he got out his telescope and surveyed behind him first and could not see Danielle and Caleb, which meant they were staying concealed, as he had told them.

When he looked to the east, he saw the ones who had made the large fire the night before and they were headed directly toward him. They were white settlers. In the lead was a small man who had a beard and was walking with a limp. He sounded just like the guide Danielle had described. He figured that the settlers were going to travel a little north of where Danielle and Caleb were located.

Crazy Runner ran back to Danielle and Caleb and immediately got them moving. They went over the ridge to a place directly in the route the settlers were traveling. He found a place for them to hide that was only about ten feet from the trail, but they would be well hidden. He explained to Danielle exactly what he wanted them to do.

Crazy Runner ran up the trail about 50 yards in the opposite direction and then started walking back down the trail. He had it planned so it would appear as though he were traveling alone in the opposite direction as the settlers. He had planned it almost perfectly. When he met the settlers on the trail, it was only about 15 feet from where Danielle and Caleb were hidden. He could tell that Owens was upset at seeing another white man.

Owens just said, "Howdy" and kept walking not wanting to stop and have this white man tell the settlers about the dangers. Crazy Runner stopped directly in front of Owens and said in a loud and friendly voice., "My name's Crazy Runner, I haven't seen another white man is a couple of weeks. What is your name?"

Owens replied, "My name is Tom Jackson. We have a lot of miles to make today, so if you will excuse us." He started to go around Crazy Runner and down the trail. Before he could take two steps one of the settlers said, "Wait a minute Tom, this man might be able to give us some information about Indian activity, since he has just come from that direction."

Owens stopped and turned to find Crazy Runner pointing his rifle at him. "What is going on?" Owens said looking at the rifle with big eyes. Crazy Runner said, "Drop your rifle and pistol on the ground." Owens started to argue when Crazy Runner cocked his rifle and then he immediately put both down on the ground.

Then Danielle and Caleb came out from their hiding place. As soon as Owens saw her, his face turned white, as though he had seen a ghost.

Danielle said, "To you he is Tom Jackson. To the group of settlers I was with about three months ago he was Colin Owens. He led us into an ambush by the Creeks and I saw a Frenchman pay him money for doing it. All of the men were killed and scalped; the surviving women and children went with the Creek to be their slaves. My son and I were taken captive by the Creeks until this man rescued us."

The settlers started staring at each other in disbelief.

Crazy Runner then walked up to Owens/Jackson, quickly pulled out his knife out of his boot, stuck it in Owens/Jackson's stomach, twisted it and pulled it out leaving him screaming in agony on the ground. He then calmly turned to the settlers and said, "If you want to stay alive follow me." He started back down the trail from where the settlers had come with Danielle and Caleb closely behind. As he passed the settlers, he counted 12 men, 7 women, and 4 children. He smiled as he remembered

CRAZY RUNNER - TRAILBLAZER - 1750

something that one of the slaves from the Violet Plantation used to say, "The day of reckoning comes to all evil men."

It took a couple of minutes for the settlers to make up their minds and they came running to catch up. About two hours later, they stopped at a stream and took a break. One of the settlers came up to Crazy Runner and said, "How do we know you are not doing exactly what you accused him of doing?"

Crazy Runner looked him straight in the eye and said, "You don't".

This answer took the man by surprise he was hoping for something a lot more reassuring.

After a few minutes the man said, "Why did you just leave him lying there screaming in agony?"

"For what he did, he did not deserve a quick death! He needed to die slowly and in as much pain as possible!"

After the man had taken this in, he asked, "Where are you leading us?"

"There is a large valley that is protected by the Cherokee, they are allowing peaceful white settlers to stay there and farm. I am taking you there, just as I led the settlers who are already there to that valley. If those settlers decide that they want you, then you can settle there. It is just over those mountains to the southeast and about a day and a half from here.

I am heading in a direction that you are fairly certain is safe. You have no idea what is going on west of here."

The man went back to other settlers to explain to them what he had been told. Danielle had already talked to the group and told them in more detail what Owens/Jackson had done, how Crazy Runner had rescued them over a week ago, the precautions he had gone to keep them safe and he was now taking them to a settlement where they would be safe.

Crazy Runner said to the group, "Because of the number of

people we are going to have to travel slowly. When I am not here Danielle Bowerman is in charge, you do exactly what she tells you, when she tells you and we will all get through this alive. I am leaving her in charge because I have already taught her how to find safe places. I am going ahead to scout. Danielle, you just follow this trail. If the trail forks, I will leave a broken branch showing you which trail to take. If you see two sticks lying across each other in an X with a third stick pointing in a direction, take them in that direction and find a place to hide."

  He took off running down the trail. Caleb wanted to go with him, but Danielle held him. Crazy Runner ran about three miles and then went up a hill and scouted in every direction. He saw a Creek scouting party on the same trail behind the settlers, but they were further back then where the settlers were when he first met them. He was hoping that Owens/Jackson was already dead and would not send them in this direction.

  He looked in all other directions and saw a new trail which lead directly toward the mountains, behind which was Hank Jacobs settlement.

  When he looked back up the trail he saw that the Creeks had indeed found Owens/Jackson and were on their trail. Danielle had the settlers traveling hard. He had been right to pick her to lead. Not only did she know how he traveled and how to find safe places, but also the men did want to seem weak and have a women travel faster than they wanted to travel.

  Crazy Runner ran full speed directly to the group. He instructed Danielle on which trail to take a couple of miles ahead. He grabbed four young men and had them follow him back they way they had just come. When they got well away from the group he stopped and explained that there was a Creek scouting party that had found Owens/Jackson and were on their trail. These Indians must be killed so they cannot go back and get more Creek warriors. He picked places for them to hide and explained who each was to shoot and he would be up the trail picking them off from behind before they got to this ambush site.

The men went to where he had told them and when he was sure they were well hidden, Crazy Runner ran up the trail about ¼ of a mile and hid himself, getting his bow and arrows ready.

Crazy Runner had earlier seen five braves. As they came down the trail, he only saw four. That meant that one of them had been sent back to tell others. As they passed his position, he killed the fourth one and the third one. The settlers shot the first two. Then he went running down the trail and the four settlers were running after him. The main group had already reached the fork and had taken the trail to the southeast as they were supposed to. Crazy Runner left one man to follow that trail and to cover the steps the others had made. He took the other three leaving a false trail to the northeast. They ran about two miles, stomping their feet heavily into the ground, making sure not to step where a man in front of them had stepped, when they came to a stream. Crazy Runner instructed the men to walk in the water downstream. He went upstream a little ways and left an obvious trail out of the water onto rocks. Then he went back into the water and went as fast as he could downstream. When he caught up to the men, he passed them and they followed him in the stream for about two miles until they came to the trail the others had taken. They had gotten to that place about the same time as the man covering the trail. All five of them took turns covering the trail for another mile. Then they ran to catch up to the group who were only a short distance ahead.

It was now late in the afternoon. Crazy Runner ran ahead to check out a very large cave for the group to spend the night. He had found this cave earlier and he wanted to make sure that there were no bears or anything else in the cave before he took the settlers there.

The cave was empty. It was a good location because there was a pool of water in the back and from the cave entrance you had a good view to the east, north, and west. It was located only about an hour's walk from the river going into the north side of the valley where Hank Jacob's settlement was located.

He went back, got the settlers and led them to the cave. Once they were inside two of the women started picking up wood and were about to start a fire. Danielle yelled, "Don't do that." One of the women screamed back, "I don't want to be cold tonight, I want a hot meal and the Indians cannot see a fire in here." Danielle answered, "They can't see the fire, but until the sun goes down they will be able to see the smoke."

Crazy Runner immediately said, "Danielle is right. We left a false trail for the Creek heading northeast. If they see smoke from here, it will lead them directly to us. It looks as though it will be a very cloudy night, so after it is full dark you can light up a fire, have a hot meal and get warm.

I am going to leave and go to that settlement. There are only two ways there. One is by river and the other is up and over this mountain. I think going over the mountain would be too hard on the children, so I am going to have people from the settlement bring rafts upstream so you can ride down the river. I will be back in the morning.

Make sure there is a guard near the entrance at all times, but stay behind that large boulder and never out in the open. Set up shifts."

He took off his pack, bow and arrows, and laid both rifles with them. He felt that his leaving his things with the settlers would comfort them that he was coming back. Then he left, but not before carefully looking around from behind the boulder at the entrance.

Chapter 49—A New Home

Running full speed, it only took Crazy Runner 15 minutes to reach the river. It took him another 15 minutes of going along the shore to find a large log. Just before he pushed the log out into the river, he gave a big wave with both hands to where he knew the lookout was. He tied his pistols and powder horn together. Then he grabbed the log, placed his pistols and powder horn on top of it and proceeded to kick his feet to move the log out to the center of the river and float through the canyon. As soon as he was through the canyon, he kicked his feet to get the log over to the far shore. It was cold in the water and he wanted to get out as soon as possible.

As soon as he had his feet on dry ground, Crazy Runner started running, because he was anxious to get warmed up and it was still over a mile to the Settlement House. There were several men around the Settlement House waiting for him when he arrived. They were very happy to see it was him.

They took him inside to warm up and he immediately started telling them about Danielle and Caleb Bowerman, Colin Owens/

Tom Jackson, and the other settlers. Hank Jacobs said that everyone would be welcome here. After he had a discussion with some of the men he added, "If they decide they want to stay, they will be most welcome to do that. What do you want us to do?"

Crazy Runner replied, "At first light we need to take several large rafts up the river to just the other side of the canyon. Then I will go and get the folks and bring them to the rafts."

Hank said, "Ok, we will do that. By the way, when we saw you earlier you were looking for Big Jim. Did you find him?"

Crazy Runner explained, "Some white men killed him for the pelts he had with him".

Hank replied, "I am very sorry to hear that. He was a good man."

"Yes, he was." Crazy Runner added.

Shortly after daybreak, they had four large rafts poling up the river. The men knew a good place to paddle over to the other side and then they poled through the canyon on that side. They landed about ½ mile past the entrance to the canyon.

Immediately, Crazy Runner took off at full speed heading for the cave. Danielle had been using his telescope and had seen the rafts. When Crazy Runner reached the cave she already had everyone packed up and ready to move out. Crazy Runner picked up his things and led them to the river, the rafts, and safety. The settlers appeared to be moving much faster today, Crazy Runner thought that the probable reason for this is that they were so close to safety.

As soon as they got to the rafts, Hank Jacobs took over. He would point to a person and tell them which raft they were to get on. They listened and promptly did exactly as he instructed. It did not take long to get everyone on board and soon they pushed off and were headed downriver.

They took the rafts all the way down to near the Settlement House. Hank Jacobs led everyone to the Settlement House while Crazy Runner helped to tie up the rafts. By the time Crazy Runner reached the Settlement House the settlers were all inside being welcomed.

He had no sooner walked in the door than Sam came up to him and gave him a big bear hug, saying, "I can't thanks you enough. These are the nicest people I's ever known. They has really accepted us as people." Crazy Runner laughed at first and then noticed that many people were looking at him and he got embarrassed at the attention.

After everyone finished eating Hank got up and said, "None of us would be here were it not for Crazy Runner. Thank you." With that, everyone started applauding. Crazy Runner's face turned beet red with the applause. Then Hank continued, "To you new people, we have this entire valley for our farms. We work together helping each other out like one big family. No man is alone here. This is Cherokee territory and we are friendly with the Cherokee; in fact, there are two Cherokee families living at the east end of the valley. In turn, the Cherokee help protect us from the Creek and Chickasaw. As long as you agree not to cause any trouble, to help your neighbors when they need it and not hunt outside of this valley, then you folks are welcome to stay here. Those of us who were here first, have farms already laid out. You new people will rest today, get to know us and let us get to know you, then tomorrow we will show you where you can pick out your farms if you decide to stay. You will stay here in our Settlement House until you have a place of your own."

One of the new settlers asked, "Who owns the slave?" pointing to Sam who was still standing next to Crazy Runner. Hank and Crazy Runner looked at each other and smiled as Hank said, "He is not a slave! All men in this valley are free men." Hank added, "He is one of us and one of the best men working with wood I have ever seen." At this, Sam got embarrassed.

Hank then took the men outside while the women stayed inside and got acquainted. Hank pointed out their lookout system and explained that everyman had to serve a six-hour rotating shift on watch at one place or the other. Then the men started visiting and getting to know one another.

The four settler children and Caleb were off playing with the other children. Crazy Runner was watching them and smiling. Danielle walked up to him and said, "This is a wonderful place. Thank you for rescuing us and bringing us here."

"You are most welcome."

"You know Caleb really likes you". Then Danielle smiled and went off to be with the other women.

Crazy Runner decided it was a good time for a run. He had already laid down his rifles, bow and arrows, and pack inside the Settlement House. He took the two pistols, put them with his other things and then headed off on a run. He ran almost the entire length of the valley. He saw the two Cherokee lodges and stopped and introduced himself, talked to them in Cherokee for a little while and then continued running.

When he got back to the Settlement House, it was beginning to get dark and everyone was just finished eating supper. He had a little of the leftovers. Danielle and Caleb had picked out a nice little place on the second floor to sleep.

Danielle walked up to Crazy Runner and said, "Let's go outside."

They walked down to the river and Danielle said, "These are very nice people. They said for awhile we will stay in the Settlement House and then the men will build us a cabin."

"So you are going to stay here. That is good news."

"Why is that good news?"

Crazy Runner did not know what she meant by this question. He paused and then said, "Because now you do not have to go back to Virginia and you have a permanent home of your own."

She looked up at him, shook her head and said, "These people are so nice, don't you want to settle down here?"

"There is still a lot out there for me to see and do."

She grabbed the back of his head, pulled his head down and kissed him. It was a long passionate kiss. This was Crazy Runner's first kiss. It scared him, but not enough to want it to stop. Then she said, "I realize I am older that you, but I will make you a good wife if you will have me."

"I...I...I..."

"Think about it." Then Danielle slowly turned and walked back to the Settlement House. Crazy Runner just stood there watching her walk away. For the first time he noticed that she was very attractive.

She stopped about ten feet away, turned back to him and said, "By the way, I was told by Hank Jacobs that your birthday is March 17, St Patrick's Day, is that correct?"

"Yes"

"Well, that is today, so Happy Birthday."

Chapter 50—A Decision

He walked around most of the night thinking. He stayed in mostly open areas so he could easily see the stars on this cloudless night. He was now 18-years-old. He was now middle-aged; because there were few people he had known who lived to be over 36.

Little Deer would have made him a good wife, but he said he did not want to settle down. Danielle has just proposed marriage to him. Was he ready to settle down? What could he do if he did settle down? He had done a lot of farming as an indentured servant; however, when he left the Violet Plantation, he had pledged to himself he would not work the land again. Danielle was definitely a wonderful, beautiful woman; he especially liked the way she had taken over with the settlers. She seemed to really like the wilderness. She was nice to look at, she certainly did kiss nice and if felt good to have her body pressed up against his, but then he did not have any experience with which to compare it.

He had been walking around for several hours and the same

thoughts keep coming into his mind repeatedly. Suddenly he was surprised when he Danielle standing right there in front of him. He stopped and just looked at her. He did not know what to say. She did not say anything either. She walked over, put her arm in his, and they walked together in silence. They walked for almost an hour with neither saying a word.

She stopped and pulled him over to a fallen tree near the river where they sat down with the moon reflecting off the water. Another half-hour went by and then Danielle said, "Will you please talk to me and tell me what you are honestly thinking? I am really sorry at being so forward, but I wanted you to know how I felt. Hank Jacobs said you would probably be leaving soon, that you never stayed very long."

"Ok. I ran away from the plantation because I didn't like being tied down. Yes, I could work the ground, but I didn't like it. I have been on my own for almost a year. I really like the freedom of traveling around. I really like seeing new things and new places. I really like you. That was the first time I have ever been kissed and I really liked it."

She got up, sat in his lap and kissed him again. This kiss was even more passionate and much longer than the first.

"I like traveling with you, but I have Caleb and we could not do that with him."

"I like you a lot, but you see I think I make a difference in this world. If it had not been for me, the settlers here in this valley would not have found this place where they could farm without worrying about being attacked by Indians. If it would not been for me Sam would probably have not found his family and definitely would not be here where he is accepted for who he is and what he can do. If it had not been for me, you might not have been rescued. If it had not been for me, then these other settlers might have gone through the same thing you did. If I am out there, I might be able to make a difference in other people's lives. So I guess my decision is that I cannot settle down with you. At least not now."

"I understand", Danielle said.

"I want to thank you for something. If it had not been for you I never would have thought of those things. I never would have realized that what I want to do with my life is help people. When I was learning to read, I read in the Bible that a man must do good for others. I am going to rest another day and night and then I am going to continue to explore and help others."

Danielle kissed him and went back into the Settlement House.

LOOK FOR FUTURE BOOKS
BY RALPH BOWMAN!

LaVergne, TN USA
08 December 2010
207930LV00001B/24/P